AN ANTHOLOGY
OF RURAL STORIES
BY WRITERS OF COLOR
2024

AN ANTHOLOGY
OF RURAL
STORIES BY
WRITERS OF
COLOR, 2024

ISBN: 978-1-958094-55-6

EastOver Press encourages the use of our publications
in educational settings. For questions about educational discounts,
contact us online: www.EastOverPress.com or info@EastOverPress.
com.

Book Design by Beste M. Doğan

10 9 8 7 6 5 4 3 2 1

Published in the United States of America by

EASTOVER PRESS
Rochester, Massachusetts
www.EastOverPress.com

EastOver
PRESS

———

an

ANTHOLOGY

of

RURAL

STORIES

by

WRITERS

of

COLOR,

2024

———

edited by

Erika T.
Wurth

TABLE OF CONTENTS

INTRODUCTION

Though I've been asked to write an introduction for an anthology of short stories, these days, I'm best known for being a horror novelist. It's almost strange to think about the nights that I used to sit in my office in the middle of the Midwest, alone, looking out the window when I needed a break from the words, the cicadas singing in the long green grass, the occasional scream of a cougar in the deep, dark, wet night.

There is something magical about them, though.

Going even further back, I remember reading the author's note

(I always read the author's note) of either Stephen King's *Night Shift* or *Different Seasons*, each of which I found wandering the school library during lunch hour, and King's saying that a short story is like a "kiss in the dark." I liked that. They are like a kiss in the dark—and if I remember correctly, though I feel that it would take some of the punch, the magic out of the thing to check, he says a kiss in the dark by a stranger. It's true. They'll hit you hard and then just as suddenly, leave you—and there's something beautiful about their simultaneous completeness and shortness. There have been short stories that have stayed with me for years, decades.

This anthology is cool. As a person of Indigenous descent who didn't grow up on the Rez, or in the city, I know what it's like to be in-between, to live in a place where your demographic might in reality proliferate, but because the outside perception of it is so opposite, it's hard for you to think of yourself as part of a collective, not that that's always ideal, if you're a writer—though community is good. When it's good.

There is so much beauty in this book. So many different stories coming from so many different rural areas, and so much rich language. Only a short number of years ago, there were so few Indigenous writers (and other BIPOC!) coming to the fore. Don't get me wrong. We were trying. We were trying to tell our stories, awkwardly, beautifully, whatever way they were coming out of us— but it was surrealistically difficult to get much in the way of attention. I know that literary writers claim to eschew it—but here's the thing: attention leads to livelihood, it leads to tenure-track jobs, advances large enough to feed the family, spend time writing the next one. It leads to yet another writer (and there are so many these last few years) who might put out a collection or a novel that will change someone's life. Another Indigenous kid in another rural area, wondering if there's anyone like them out there. So, forgive me if I put a premium on attention, as long as it's not the only goal.

In any case, I hope you love these as much as I did.

ERIKA T. WURTH, 2024

an

ANTHOLOGY

of

RURAL

STORIES

by

WRITERS

of

COLOR,

2024

BRAND
NEW
PLAGUES

---

by
RON AUSTIN

A mean hex mutated every sorry scrap of junk inside Three Kings Pawnshop. Merchandise took on nasty animalistic aspects. Nothing could be salvaged. Best believe me. I'm saying slimy water hoses slithered and shed snake skin. Microphones grew burly gorilla fur. Cordless power drills bucked warthog tusks. Tangled beef guts exploded from microwaves like spring-loaded confetti. Leaf blowers whipped thick elephant trunks. Braided gold chains flexed tough body builder veins. The sound of old folks coughing crackled from phlegm-spitting bass speakers. Blood and snot splattered clean display cases. Beast stink head-butted my nose. I peeped that repugnant mess and bugged out. I'd been a grunt slash bodyguard and more at Three Kings for forever. A ruined pawnshop would ruin me. I couldn't afford to change lanes and start over. I prayed for forgiveness and chain-smoked three cigarettes back to back to back. But Effie, The High and Mighty Miss Boss Lady, didn't trip.

Since Miss Boss Lady was the new owner of Three Kings, she had to prove herself competent. She couldn't flinch at high-powered hood shit, fist fights, attempted robberies, or crooked-ass cops—it looked like she wouldn't let supernatural assaults break her back either. Bargain bin black magic could be copped at any corner store in this time of signs and wonders. Canned sacrificial lamb, extra-strength antifungal atonement ointment, and everlasting sardine tins sat next to snacks and aspirin. Any chump could cast a brutal spell quicker than popping popcorn, smack enemies with festering boils. Though this shit was brand new.

Salty poltergeists swaggered inside big screen TVs. Designer purses pursed unrepentant lips. Brain matter clouded cubic zirconia. Antique revolvers sneezed gunpowder. Disgruntled chainsaws growled threats. Shelves rattled, and Effie didn't say boo. She didn't stumble, didn't sweat out her finger waves, didn't drop her clipboard, didn't bust one wrinkle in her frumpy, armor-plated blazer. She kept right on taking inventory with that tired look on her face, as if it was any other Saturday morning, as if beetle-winged brooches weren't circling her head. I couldn't believe that fronting-ass, phony-baloney act.

To tell the whole truth, I never liked Effie from the jump. I tried advising Miss Wannabe after she inherited Three Kings from Uncle Zeke, lord rest his trifling, rotten, greedy soul (the man would've snatched his own grandmama's wig, braided it, dyed it, and sold it right back to her). As she was the niece of the man who employed me for years, I felt obliged to show her the basics, hip her to that good game. I told her to think about expansion and real money moves, flipping payday loans and classic cars. She hit me back with every buzzword she learned from earning a degree in non-profit management. Ungrateful as could be, she rattled off nonsense about social equity and ethical businesses. Next she told me possibly the third dumbest thing I've ever heard in my life: she told me she didn't want more profit; she wanted to turn Three Kings into a secondhand shop slash low-key charity, decked out with a canned-good drive, debt-forgiveness, and educational seminars on economics and building generational wealth.

Now I didn't get disrespectful. I didn't talk over her head. But I did keep it real. I told her what Zeke told me—nobody likes pawnbrokers. This is the business of the quick and the dead. Pawnbrokers cut steak from misfortune, crunch pennies out of family heirlooms, and no amount of good will can spark cold furnaces, bend prison bars, restart dead engines, cast out cancer, or replace the dollar almighty. Amen. I offered to hash out our differing life philosophies over a bottle of Paul Masson at Empire Lounge, but she wouldn't listen to what I had to say. She told me *fraternization between management and employees would be untenable at best.* Then she put that extra little funk on it, talked about organizational restructuring, and had the nerve to make it sound like I was lucky to keep my goddamn job. Ain't that about a bitch.

Effie didn't respect me, and I couldn't blame her. She didn't know how I came up off the muscle. She didn't know me back from when I used to rock rat-eaten t-shirts and socks, back when I used to mow lawns for nothing but a damn can of frank and beans, back when I scraped change out of the gutter, back when I used to chew cuticles bloody, back when roaches squatted in my sneakers, back when I had to teach myself the oldest, truest magic—how to turn something out of nothing, pull a dollar out of fifteen cents. On God. It's easy for folks to mistake a career pawnshop grunt as shiftless, as a man who turns whatever he touches into trash. It's easy to be overlooked, and I thought about making her see me. I thought about quitting in a rage, cussing her out, spitting on her polished shoes. But I bit my tongue and let it be. I know the smart man has got to go along to get along, even if it rips out his goddamn heart.

Funny thing is, scripture says God's disfavor has a way of visiting the high and mighty. His good wrath appeared in the flesh at Three Kings Pawnshop. Silver bracelets caterpillar-crawled, bruised cellphones doubled-over with cramps, hotplates frothed hog fat, and there she was, Miss Better Than You, stunting on me like a mother-fucker. She didn't cry, didn't crack. Any other trout-mouthed sucker would've at least asked *how did this junk get up and grow legs?* But she couldn't be bothered.

I needed her to face this predicament head on, and so I got at her like this: I snatched a beetle-winged brooch out of the air and pinched its wings between my fingertips. Scratchy insect legs struggled. A gold-plated stinger jerked and oozed milky venom. Lifeblood beat inside dark rubies. I shoved that monstrosity under her nose and hollered, "Jesus, Joseph, and Mary—Miss Boss Lady, ain't this something else?"

Effie looked at the monster, looked at me, and then swatted my hand. She double-downed and asked me, "What am I supposed to do with this junk now?"

"You've got to be joking."

She jabbed her pen at a fanged pair of pliers. Those pliers snapped and spat sparks. She jumped back and frowned. She told me, "I don't have time for jokes. I don't have time for a damn thing."

I threw that beetle-winged brooch on the floor and stomped it. It splattered good like a water bug. I lit up another cigarette and told her dumbass, "You say what you s'posed to do with this junk? Hell, ain't you s'posed to be selling it?"

"James, you know I'm not out here trying to be slick. It's not about lost profits. It's about honoring our contracts. Folks have their whole lives wrapped up in this junk."

"Yes you is, Miss Boss Lady. You is slick—you slicker than a can of Crisco bumping uglies with a catfish."

"James—I told you don't call me that."

"Don't call you what? I'm saying you cold, cold-blooded with that hustle game. Don't doubt yourself." I searched the shelves and found a scabby flashlight. It looked safe enough to handle. A yellow, infected eyeball blinked where the lens should've been. Stiff eyelashes fluttered. One crusty eyelid drowsed. I clicked the switch. The flashlight twitched. The eyeball teared up and released a weak, watery beam. I placed the flashlight under my chin and modeled a creature-feature pose. "See what I'm saying, Miss Boss Lady? This thing can still put in work. Don't throw the baby out with the bathwater."

She pushed me out of the way and continued taking inventory. She told me. "James, you need to stop calling me Miss Boss Lady."

I pointed the light at her back. Wrinkles broke the seam of her blazer. Sweet sweat collected at the nape of her neck. I told her, "I don't mean no disrespect, Effie. You should be less worried about me and more worried about whoever slapped us with this bullshit." She turned and studied me the same way she studied the shelves, appraising the worth in my raggedy old bones. I beamed that weak, watery light in her face. She winced and raised a defensive hand. A tear slipped from the flashlight's eye, fell warm on my hand. I asked her, "Who do you think did it?"

She shook her head. "Shoot, I don't know. You're the one who said it—nobody likes a pawnbroker. Nobody liked my grimy old uncle. Nobody likes me. It could've been anybody and nobody at all. It could've been a kid or somebody late on their payments. It could've been you for all I know."

I aimed that flashlight at the ceiling and traced figure eights. "Nuh-unh. Don't throw them pissy sheets on me. I'm a fool, but not the type of fool that'd cut off his nose to spite his face. I don't clown like that, Miss Boss Lady. No Ma'am."

"James, quit playing with me."

"You the one running game."

"I told you don't call me Miss Boss Lady."

"It's all good, Effie. You are the boss. I am but a humble servant."

"You ain't shit, James. You know that, right?

"Wait a minute, wait a goddamn minute! Miss Boss Lady—I thought we was professionals. Ain't this what they call harassment? Defamation of character? Or is it retaliation? Don't fool around and make me report you to the corporate office."

"James, let me say it again—you ain't shit."

"You sho'll right. I ain't shit. I ain't been shit since the day I was born. But see, that's the difference between you and me—I ain't gotta lie to nobody."

After talking all that weak-ass trash, Miss Boss Lady got heated, tore off that frumpy, armor-plated blazer, rolled up her sleeves, wrapped up her finger waves, and barked orders. She commanded me to corral, restrain, and store every docile, gross, and aggressive item noted in the inventory. I knotted slithering water hoses

Three Kings Inventory

1. Good
2. Docile
3. Gross
4. Aggressive
5. Dangerous

Personal Information	
Owner	Euphimia Elaine Spivey
Address	55 N. Grand Avenue
City, State, ZIP	St. Louis, Mo. 63108
Phone	314-325-6088

Item	Description	Condition	Est. Value
Hand bag	GG Marmont mini, top handle	Has developed pouting lips 2 Docile	Worthless
Revolver	Smith + Wesson model 19, classic	Runny muzzle, sneezing, common cold accidental discharge possible 5 Dangerous	corrupt
Bass Speaker	JBL PB 2000 subwoofer	coughing + hacking, phlegm sounds like bronchitis 3. Gross	infected
Axe	Husqvarna 2611, wooden handle	(Good)	priceless
LCD Television	Toshiba 48" Tru-color technology	Haunted??? Possessed? 4. Aggressive	N/A

into bows, chucked mutated power tools into dog cages, muzzled phlegm-spitting bass speakers, body-slammed bleeding microwaves into trash cans, and locked that bedeviled junk away in the basement. I did all the heavy lifting while Effie organized a few items unaffected by the hex, a shovel, two axes, a handful of hammers. My back hurt by the time we were through—and to add injury to injury—I got bit by that pair of fanged pliers. Motherfucker took meat off my knuckles. Miss Manager Of The Century didn't even get the first aid kit. It was all good though. I bandaged the wound myself, thugged it out.

By the time I finished mopping guts up off the floor and bleaching the counters, Camille showed up for her shift. To tell the whole truth, I didn't like Camille either. She was one of Miss Boss Lady's enlightened collegiate associates who helped spearhead structural reorganization at Three Kings. The woman ate vegan bacon, never washed her nappy dreads, babbled nonsense about the divine feminine, used organic baking soda for deodorant, and mooched my cigarettes like it was a religion. She peeped the aftermath of that repugnant mess and smoked three of my cigarettes back to back to back.

I shrugged and said, "They got us."

Camille asked, "Who?"

I said, "Who knows?"

Miss Boss Lady said, "Does it matter? We got work to do."

Me and Miss Boss Lady agreed for once, and I told her, "You sho'll right. There is work to do. Let me rap with you right quick. First, I gotta ask you this—don't they teach y'all to think outside the box? See y'all be paying all that good money out the yang-yang for a piece of paper just to get stuck on stupid."

Cigarette smoke haloed Camille's head. She copped this attitude and said, "What the fuck is you saying?"

The bite wound ached, but I had a lecture to give. I told Miss Boss Lady and Camille, "Problems become opportunities with the right perspective. This junk might be dead ugly—but I'm saying this is the time of sign and wonders—we could make a killing off this bullshit."

Camille and Boss Lady mean-mugged me. I continued my pontification on basic supply and demand, but before I could finish, three loud thumps came from Miss Boss Lady's back office. THUMP! THUMP! THUMP! That's where she kept food drive donations, including two mini-fridges full of flour and sugar, bricks of shrimp-flavored ramen, and a pyramid of canned goods. The thumping came again—THUMP! THUMP! Camille muttered *fuck this shit* under her breath. I threw up my hands. Miss Boss Lady shook her head and investigated. She stepped to the door, turned that knob, peeked inside.

Inside the back office, rubbery pink octopus tentacles shot out from cans of spam and thrashed—but that ain't it. That's not what did the thumping. It was the two mini-fridges. They had grown thick power lifter arms and legs. They blundered like drunks, swung swollen fists, and bashed holes in the drywall. A quick tentacle whipped at Miss Boss Lady's head. She swayed back and then slammed the door shut. Worry rippled her brow. Her chest heaved. I caged a mean, satisfied laugh in my throat. I thought she was about to sob and rip her hair out. Tear at her breast. But she didn't. She recovered her composure, broke a fake smile, and said, "It looks like there's no rest for the wicked."

I couldn't goddamn believe it. In one day Miss Boss Lady lost her family business and she didn't have the natural-born decency to hang her head in shame and ask *why me? Who hates me this much?* Man, I could've shot her dead right there on the spot. But every gun in the place sniffled and would need a dose of Robitussin before firing a single, snot-slicked bullet. I played it cooler than Eskimo piss in a blizzard, bit my tongue, and fronted just the same. I threw up my hands and said, "Effie, if you don't mind, I need a break to get my head right. This foolishness got me beat, you hear me? Beat."

ALRIGHT—FUCK IT. Y'ALL GOT ME DEAD TO RIGHTS.
OF COURSE I CAST THAT GODDAMN HEX.
IT AIN'T NO BIG FAT STINKING SECRET.

For real for real. I did it after a long night of drinking and scheming on reconciliation. I had tried to sacrifice my pride, lay my head low, and play a role, but Effie never did respect my efforts, and to tell the truth, I never did respect her ambitions. I thought about how to get us back on the right foot as I slugged shots of Paul Masson at Empire Lounge. By the fifth shot, fresh blood flowed into my head, and I realized my mistake. The fault in our professional relationship wasn't a matter of respect. It was a matter of need. She'd never want me, but I could make her need me.

I settled my tab, hit Family Dollar, and between necropolis calling cards and cans of carbonated oxblood, I found Kid Pharaoh's

Premium Hella Hexes Curse Kits. I picked the Biblical Classics Pack and stumbled my trifling-ass home. The Biblical Classics Pack promised to unleash personalized versions of Egyptian-inspired plagues. I followed the instructions, spat venom in that single-use, aluminum cauldron, and fantasized about Miss Boss Lady blighted by my hand, about her covered in painful boils, about her blinded, about her snake bit, about her begging for my help. I'd pop those boils, soothe her sores, heal her, make her whole again. When it was all said and done, she'd have new faith in me. A beautiful working relationship would flourish.

Now I bought the Biblical Classics Pack for a reason. I needed Miss Boss Lady to suffer value-brand affliction that would pass as quickly as it set in. I didn't want mutant merchandise; I didn't want to run Three Kings out of business. Fucking up the money is original sin, deserving of dismemberment and death—that goes double if you fuck up your own money. I'm saying that curse kit hit me with that old bait and switch. I couldn't have that.

On my little fifteen-minute break, I lit a cigarette, dug the curse kit instructions out of my back pocket, found the customer service number, huddled over a pay phone, and fixed my mouth to complain. That phone rang for forever, and I damn near forgot why I even bothered calling. Cleaning up that repugnant mess at Three Kings took more out of me than I had thought. Sore muscles knotted fists. Exhaustion chewed my bones. That killer mid-July heat didn't help. Atomic sunlight charred worms. Molten asphalt belched toxic fumes. My blood sizzled and popped inside my skin like fish grease. By the time a young lady finally answered and started talking her talk, I wanted to fall out. But I was too salty and frustrated to quit.

I jawed about the bum hex and how I got cheated. I demanded she reverse the curse and refund me for my troubles to boot. I threw a bit of extra funk on it and said, "And you know the worst part about it? I been gassing this woman up all day, rubbing it in her face, and nothing. She ain't crying. Not a tear. None of this shit is breaking her back. I can't even get the satisfaction of seeing her suffer, and it's driving me, boy, is it driving me."

The young lady started reading a script and told me, "I'm sorry to hear our product failed to meet expectations. But if you had read the included product disclaimer, you'd understand that magical solutions are more art than science and cannot guarantee specific outcomes according to the caster's transgressive intent. For example, stupefying hallucinations may occur as a symptom of concurrent fever due to hexing and may not act as a standalone bane. Furthermore, Catacombs Incorporated cannot be held liable for any karmatic repercussions caused by the malicious use of Quick Curse technology."

"See that's what I mean about bait and switch," Her corporate talk made my head hurt, and I lost my train of thought. Quartz sparked in broken sidewalk slabs. Gnats nipped my ears. Sticky blood seeped down the back of my hand. I shook my head clear and kept arguing. "The box promised blisters, boils, gnats, all that good stuff."

"Banes described in marketing language are approximations and do not reflect concrete applications or outcomes. A wide range of unique manifestations are possible. Can you tell me more about the items in your pawnshop? Most importantly, are these items that you're familiar with? That you've touched?"

The blood came faster, soaked my bandage, trickled through my fingers. I kept up my charm and answered the young lady. "Why yes ma'am, I haul the junk in, I haul the junk out. Everything on them shelves got my stink on it."

"Since casting the hex, have you been feeling irritable? Confused? Frustrated? Are you experiencing feelings of dread? Hopelessness? Self-loathing? Have you been drinking and smoking more?"

"Yes, yes, yes, and yes. The good doctor slapped me in my face and called my mama ugly on the day I was born—tell me what's new."

"Have you experienced prophetic dreams or premonitions? Have you received visits from spirits, malicious or otherwise?"

"No—nothing funny like that."

"One more question—this concerns the receiver of the hex. Were you angry with them?"

"What kind of question is that? What do you think?"

"Sir, I'll ask again—are you angry with the receiver of the curse? Take your time and think."

That bite wound ached, and I had to steady my breath. Blood seeped through the bandage. I tasted battery acid on my tongue. I gripped the phone harder and said, "When you put it like that, I guess no. I'm not mad at whoever. If I'm mad at anybody, I'm mad at me. Sometimes you get so tired of being pathetic you don't know what else to do. Now tell me what that means."

"Sir, I'm afraid you might be experiencing the onset of karmatic blowback. Before moving forward, I suggest you read the product disclaimer and—"

I figured the jig was up, and I already know what she had to say, so I hung up on that young lady, crumpled the hex instructions, and headed back to Three Kings. My petty misdeed of pride and envy grew teeth and came back to chew on my ass. There wasn't anything left to do but confess and keep moving.

<u>Disclaimer</u>
**All casters assume risk of receiving karmatic blowback. If you seek to blind enemies, you forfeit your eye to arrow and razor edge. If you seek to silence enemies, you forfeit your tongue to grinder and fang. If you seek to crack crowns, you forfeit your skull to hammer and cudgel.

Camille sat on the stoop outside Three Kings looking defeated and straight stupid. She wore a black trash bag drenched in stinking slop. Chunks of gristle smattered her dreadlocks. Old girl looked up at me, and I didn't have the heart to talk greasy. I gave her my last cigarette, lit it for her too, and asked, "What's cracking?

"Effie done lost her goddamn mind, that's what's cracking. Go see for yourself." She blew out a stream of smoke. "It ain't pretty."

Effie was hard-working, educated, and successful, somebody that'd make you shrivel with envy. I'd come to understand that she was wise, too. Before reopening Three Kings under her leadership, she negotiated a fat insurance policy. It provided enough money to cover the cost of handing out payments for lost items and remodeling Three Kings into a community center, the type of place you could grab a meal and learn about hedge fund investments in the same day. I also came to understand Effie was thorough in everything she did. In order to collect the highest amount on that policy, every sorry scrap of mutated merchandise needed to be destroyed.

I stepped inside Three Kings ready to confess my transgressions and peeped Effie putting in that work. She swung a steel axe and carved up every sorry piece of that corrupted scrap. She crushed cartilage and bone. She severed muscles and tendons. Blood spurted and splashed her clothes, ruined her finger waves, and she couldn't be bothered. She didn't break. She didn't cry. After splitting a writhing water hose clean in two, she turned, and came at me with that steel axe in hand. I not ashamed to say I wanted it. I wanted her to split my skull and leave my worthless brains on the linoleum. Cleave shining spirit from unclean flesh. I wanted to be punished and absolved of my foolishness. But it wouldn't be that easy. Instead of giving me a quick death, she gave me a hammer, and said, "James, it's time to back up all that tough talk. Let's hit hard and hit it fast, and you better not say one word about being tired. Not one word."

LIVE BIRTH

by

VENITA BLACKBURN

Nell had three children before she had a say in the matter. Then she had six more. Because she was so good at childbirth and liked to walk between houses deep in the woods even when she had no business at all among the pines, the town made her a midwife. The women there weren't allowed in the hospitals, so they gave birth over straw, standing up, in their own homes. Most of the births were fine though not all, but every baby smelled fine once the odor of metal and salt was washed away. Nell didn't remember the fine babies, only the others like the one born blind and quiet yet full alive, some stillborn or breach. Another came out backwards and hairy as a cat.

One mother made it to the city and saw a film with a woman lying in a bed, giving birth to the devil. Nell too heard stories. There was supposedly a boy born with five hands and no face, his little cries locked up in his throat like bees. But that mother didn't care about bees or the devil or hands piled on to a wrist like petals, just the bed. She didn't want to stand up to deliver her child. Nell told her when fruit falls from a tree it falls down not sideways. Which is easier dropping a sack of flour or throwing it across the room? The woman just blinked and let her mouth hang open, and Nell thought this must be how the baby happened to her too.

When there were no bellies to check on Nell still took her walks. Her husband didn't say much but sometimes seized her by the elbow and said, "there ain't nothing in the trees for you." She'd pull away and go on.

Her sons left town and came back. Her daughters got degrees and got fat. The hearts of two sons stopped for good a year apart. She walked between houses through winter and spring for as long as she could, then borrowed a horse until she bought her own.

One baby was born almost a boy and almost a girl, so like God she declared one over the other for the parents to believe forever. Often there were more fingers and toes than ten and twenty. She fixed it for five dollars, tied a string around the extra finger and pulled it tight until it separated from the rest of the hand like clay.

When they took her midwife's license, the mothers in town went to the hospital and paid more money than they had to men that didn't know their names and sometimes died for all the trouble. Nell divorced her husband, gave her horse to one of their sons, and planted string beans, rutabagas, collards, and mustard greens too. Grandmothers brought their granddaughters to Nell mostly for good luck. They wanted to know things would be ok. Nell only said, "my melons don't grow in June like they used to, and the seasons never felt like this before."

There was a birth a long time ago that Nell rarely mentioned but dreamed of often. The mother listened, obeyed Nell's instructions for months, and did her part well on the critical day of labor. In two hours the child was free. When it arrived Nell couldn't give the baby to the mother, just wrapped it up quick hoping it made no sound, afraid of what that sound might be. When the mother saw Nell's face in the fading light among the scent of sweat and blood and fig blossoms, they both knew then how some things expected, longed for, hunted in our minds have been lost to us for a long time.

$$\underline{\qquad\qquad}$$

DOG

$$\underline{\qquad\qquad}$$

by
ERIN BROWN

When a man like me has been on the run as long as I have, you get to feeling like maybe this new place you stumbled on is far enough away that you could stay, maybe for a while, just keeping to yourself, you know. And then you settle down and make a home and make a mistake and make a scene and flee the scene, and you're on the run again, wondering *why* you were stupid enough to stop in the first place. Of course, somebody like me never runs out of stupid, I always keep a little extra in my shirt pocket just in case. But one day you run out of thinking maybe there's a place for you to rest, I mean really rest, someplace where you might choose not to start any trouble, where you won't be alone, man, just for a little while. I had given up. I was too tired. And that's where my head was when I found that orchard.

I'd been on the run so long at that point that it felt more like I was on-the-crawl, on my last gasp, burning to death in the highway desert morning sun. When the air has been waving like a sea for that many hours a day for that many days in a row, you don't trust your eyes when that line of green appears, when it grows. You don't trust it until you are only a few feet away and you can *smell* the shade. The ground was dry but cool, crumbly under them trees, and a water hose lay a few rows in, hooked up to a sprinkler spraying metallic-tasting water. I drank till I nearly burst, soaked my crusty clothes in the water, and dragged myself off deeper into the trees to find a nice piece of dirt to nap in.

I smelled him before I saw him, and, considering the state of my own stink, I wouldn't have thought it possible. He was in coveralls and a pair of boots even more broken down than mine, had a face that made his boots look pretty. He was a scarecrow with mange and scurvy and probably gophers and two or three plagues. Behind him was a ... I mean, I guess you could call it a dog. Thing was all over white fur, long and shiny clean straight white fur that brushed all the way to the ground even though it was tall, and two black button eyes that shone in its narrow head. I'd seen dogs like that on TV, but never in real life, and never seen one escorted by anything like that yellow-eyed, rotten-toothed scab-skinned vagrant shuffling over to where I lay. The dog stood back a ways back behind him, it's silky head low and eyes unblinking, and watched its master approach me with a broke-shaft pitchfork in his hands.

I thought I'd start the conversation off peaceful. "I was just leavin'."

He turned his face to set one wide runny eye on me and said, "You looking at my dog?"

"Nope," I said, getting to my aching feet slowly, in case he got any ideas regarding that pitchfork. "Just leavin'. Pretty trees you got here. This your land?"

"Just get on out," the man said, and sure, why not? Of course, that was easier said than done. I walked carefully away, got out of the shade (the man following me slow to the edge of the trees with that pitchfork, his dog creeping quietly behind him, head hung low), and I got back into the sun. It had reached late afternoon full searing power, and I had to make a decision on which would kill me faster, the heat or the pitchfork. Watching that crusty old crazy walk back into that gorgeous dim under the leaves, I knew I could outrun him, even on empty and with my bootsoles flapping loose from my feet, and as for the dog, as low as it was hanging its head, I had a funny feeling that it had been kicked enough times to be scared of its own shadow. Why anybody would hurt a thing that pretty—well, but the man was clearly a ways far gone. And Lord knew, men will hurt a pretty thing on occasion, for his own reasons. I'm not a one to throw stones. So, I walked the road just long enough for the man to fade back into his trees, walked a minute more, and then turned back into the trees again. The shade was dusty sweet, and if it came down to it, that man was going to let me have a rest there one way or another. I didn't feel like dying that day, and while plenty of people in my past had thought I should die before I was ready to, none of them lasted very long against me.

But I try not to think of those people. Or their families. It's too heavy to carry, you got to leave those things behind you.

The trees on this side of the orchard had little green fruit in them, hard and sour, but something is better than nothing. I ate a few, and sat back against a tree; I was asleep before the tree bark even scratched my back. I was dead asleep, the kind you can feel, when you are aware somewhere down in your soul, like you're there and wondering if you're gonna wake up out of this one. Woke up just fine, though, to the sight of a pitchfork being swung right at my stomach.

Damn thing's tips caught me and ripped what was left of my shirt; it stung like hell. I tried to leap up quick, but part of me was still running slow up out of that soul-deep sleep, so I stumbled up and squared off with Old Crazy. He looked worse in the dim, and maybe it was just an illusion, but that pretty dog behind him, watching from behind a tree, it seemed to glow. It caught my eye, and that made me pause, and that made Old Crazy even crazier.

And he yells, "YOU LOOKIN' AT MY DOG?" like I'd actually done something. My head was still sleep-fogged, but my chest stung where he got me and I was pissed, so I yelled back "YOU RIPPED MY SHIRT!" which, I don't know, I was tired, I couldn't think of much else to say.

Well, he went for me again. And that's never a good idea. I know quite a few folks who would tell you if they still could, that going after me isn't wise. He was strong, junkie strong, screaming and scratching and swinging, but he was relying on that pitchfork, and once I got up under it, it wasn't hard. And I forgot to stop, just like I always seem to do. Poor dog watched me do it. And I'm sorry for that, I will always be sorry for that.

No dog should have to see something like what I did.

It's never easy for me, after. I lost what little fruit I had eaten in a rush of stomach acid. I kicked the pitchfork away from me. I looked down at the mess of a man, and then I looked back up at the dog.

It eased forward a little, black button eyes shining, paws silent somewhere under all that glossy white hair. It sniffed the foot of Old Crazy for a moment. Then it looked up at me, black eyes shining, and gave a little tail wag.

The guilt washed out of me, all the way out. The poor thing, it was glad to see its master go. I wondered what sort of life it had been living, here in the orchard with smelly Old Crazy. It must have been a hungry life, it must have been just *starving*. I stood feeling like

I'd been reborn in a tail wag, watching that beautiful dog take Old Crazy's foot in its mouth and drag it backwards into the darkness of the trees.

It took a while for the sounds of ripping wet crunches to stop bothering me long enough to go after that dog. I got lost in those dark trees, but I knew I was getting close when I started tripping over old bones, somewhere far from the road. The leaves grew in too thick overhead to let in much starlight, but when I found the dog it was lit up like the moon had sent her beams to shine down on that dog and nothing else in the world. The thin tip of its muzzle was stained blackish, but the rest of it was just, just *perfect* white. I tried to get close, but if I got anywhere closer than five feet from it, the dog would stop chewing and dip its head and make its black button eyes go so sad it tore at my soul, and it would whimper like an un-oiled hinge. Plus, too close and I got a view of what was left of Old Crazy. He wasn't nice to look at, not that he ever was. My stomach was angry enough as it was, it didn't need to see that sight.

I fell asleep leaning against a tree, watching the dog eat, delicately tearing, silently chewing, black button eyes on me. I fell asleep in its glow, in its eyes.

The next morning, I was like a new man; a man with a place to stop, to relax, to heal a bit from the endless running. There was nothing left to convince me to abandon the orchard, and the cool early air was good on my sunburnt skin. There were more green fruits, more tin-flavored hose water, more shade and soft crumbly dirt. But the dog was hiding somewhere, and I nearly lost my mind trying to find it. Old Crazy was a dark stain under some trees and not much else; a few tacky bones flung around. But I walked around chasing every rustle of leaves, every beam of sunlight, every flicker of movement out of the corner of my eye until I was nearly lost in those trees, looking for that dog. I found the pitchfork and picked it up; I'm not sure why at first, but it made a decent walking stick when my feet started aching.

I got so tired. I was worried. The sun was setting. I could hear it snuffling, but I couldn't find it anywhere. Then suddenly my ear caught a new sound, and I was running through the trees, bootsoles nearly tearing off, and found myself skidding to a stop at the sudden appearance of a different road. The setting sun light hurt my eyes, and I heard a cry, and I had a sudden horror- was it the dog? Was it crying? Had something happened?

It wasn't the dog. On the side of the road was a car, a red car, so red it was almost bleeding its color into the air around it. Its hood was up and steam was coming out; didn't look too serious. But the ladies, two ladies, two very young women, all loose hair and sunglasses and bare skin in the pink light, were standing on the other side of the car, open-mouthed gawking at me.

It occurred to me that I must be a sight. The pitchfork gouges under my torn-open shirt itched horribly, and that was just the latest of my charms. But I thought of Old Crazy, and I got concerned, for these ladies stuck alone by the side of the road.

So I said "I'd hurry up if I were you. There's bad men around here."

One of them, one of those girls, she put her hands up all slow, said something, I can't remember what, it didn't matter all that much to me. But it was the other one, stupid girl, I saw her come around the car real slow, toward me, she took her sunglasses off, put them on her head, and crouched down all low. She held a hand out, toward me, but like toward my feet. Then I realized she was looking past me.

I turned around and saw it. Saw its sad, black eyes. Saw its glow. Saw it crouching, head low, staring up at me from a few yards away, looking helpless and scared as ever.

Don't ever let anything you love look at you like that. You'll tear the world in half to make them happy, help them hold their head up higher. And I've torn some things up, for sure, there's people in my past that would tell you, if they could. I was so tired. I didn't want to run again. Old Crazy, that wasn't my fault. I wouldn't leave here, not for anything. I had more than myself to think about now, as a man should have in his life. I had something that depended on me, something to give selflessly to. I could be a good man again. I was home.

So I turned back to those girls, and I said, "Get outta here. And quit looking at my dog."

____

THE
RABBIT
SISTERS

____

by
CARIDAD COLE

I could hear her shuffling about in the room next to mine. There were sounds of heavy breathing and of heavy clothing being dropped. Her feet lightly stuck to the floorboards as she willed her body to remain a whisper in the night. I imagined what she was doing. Reading, I thought. A door was relentlessly creaking open and closed in an indecisive rhythm. My eyelids fluttered in time although I was fixated on the wall between us. Glancing up, I saw it was nearly four in the morning. Had I had the nerve, I would have risen myself to go into the bathroom, just to sneak a glance into her bedroom. There was only so much I could piece together through sounds, and I enjoyed picturing what my sister might be doing while the rest of the house was sleeping. She was always doing the unusual thing, it seemed. I rolled over and continued listening.

There was a pause in the sounds as she heard me stirring, and suddenly I was terrified that I was ruining her fun. She didn't know that I did this most nights until I fell asleep. There wasn't anything else to do late at night in a foster home, and I felt that she was living in such a different world than I was. She had cloths hanging down from her ceiling, draping over her bed like a royal chamber, books lining the walls, stacks of journals filled with secrets. I was accustomed to being on the outside of it all, but that didn't stop me from wondering. I hugged my blankets a bit tighter when I heard her feathery tiptoe enter my room and approach my bedside. I would have liked to think she was just checking on me, but I knew she was only confirming that I still wasn't the wiser. And I wasn't. As she backed out of my room, I squeezed my eyes shut in an attempt to summon sleep once again. Before it took me, I heard a faint crash outside like a bird landing in the leaves.

When I opened my eyes once more, it was seven o'clock on Christmas morning. The house was still and waiting for me to rouse everyone for the occasion. I thought about yelling everyone's names through the house or maybe jumping on top of them until they gave in. My sister was first. A grin spread across my face as I entered her room. I assumed my attack position, her name poised on my lips.

But the state of her room was pure chaos. I padded over to her bed. A pillow was missing. I followed a blanket trail to her closet where the door was flung open and everything was spilling out. Clothing and books, stuffed animals and music, all the things I wasn't allowed to touch. I stared down at the mess, frozen. Her room was frigid and an unwelcomed, icy air was drifting in through a window that did not immediately appear to be open. I felt like a real detective, inspecting a crime scene. I pretended to talk into a walkie-talkie.

"Looks like we got a classic case of teenage negligence. Oh yes, a real slob, Nancy. Better call for backup."

I dragged one fingertip over the windowsill to check for dust and fingerprints when I noticed that the screen had been pushed out of the frame. It dangled down on the outside of the house. I looked at it for another minute and then looked around again. My sister was gone. I thought about screaming the news through the house, but I knew she wouldn't like that. She was always telling me to be cool, just be cool. So instead, I walked back through the room, reaching for the doorknob when something caught my eye once again. Her stack of journals, the sacred pillar of her entire being, was still intact in the corner of the room. It was surrounded by knocked-over books and forgotten cups lolling on their sides, but the stack itself was pristine. This was my chance. Just a peek, and I could learn so much.

I quickly glanced over both shoulders before tiptoeing over, my shaking hand hovering above the tattered cover of the topmost notebook. "1996" was sprawled across the black leather, followed by a dash to indicate it still had pages to fill. I picked it up, clutched it to my chest, and didn't know what to do next. Someone upstairs was moving around now, turning on the tap that clanked through the pipes right above our bedrooms. I ran back to my room, as if I didn't know what day it was or what had happened, slipped the journal underneath my pillow, and tricked myself into falling back asleep.

• • •

I was forced awake again by the ringing of the doorbell echoing through the house. I squinted my eyes open and saw that the sun was now directly over the trees outside my window. A smile spread over my face as I remembered it was Christmas morning and surely everyone was awake by now. I wrapped my quilt around myself and flew to my door to yank it open, only to immediately shut it inches from being closed.

Officer Paul was standing in the living room, talking to Janice and Marco, all of them with their arms crossed. Was it time for me leave already? No, I thought, because then Kelly the social worker would be here too. I crouched down to spy on them.

"Good morning and Merry Christmas, folks," said Officer Paul.

"Good morning. Did you find her?"

"No, sir. I'm sorry to tell you she wasn't out in Fireman's Field like the last time."

"Oh Marco, this is so not good. She has the savings," Janice loudly whispered as she folded into her husband. "I don't suppose you found our twenty thousand dollars? Maybe in a bag she dropped in the dark?"

"No ma'am. No bags have been found yet." Officer Paul paused, considering his boundaries. "Might I add, it's not such a great idea to keep that kind of cash just lying around, especially in a house full of bad kids."

I wasn't a bad kid. I was spying on a grown-up conversation, but I wasn't a bad kid.

Marco sighed and rubbed his wife's shoulders. "It wasn't just lying around. It was in a safe place."

"Okay," said Officer Paul, "Well, then I'll leave you all to your Christmas morning, and you can expect a call if we find anything. Listen, a girl like that, she'll be back in no time. She just turned fourteen, right? She'll be wanting her bed soon. Trust me."

Marco and Janice wordlessly showed him out.

"You know she ransacked the presents, too?" Marco told Janice. "She got the rabbit. I mean, it was for her obviously, but God, that girl. I swear. Do we not give her everything she wants? Where does she think she's going?" Janice nodded in general agreement, but the rest of their conversation was telepathic after that.

I prepared to feign ignorance of the whole situation, and started searching for my slippers beneath the quilt. But there, halfway under my bed, was a handwritten note on a page ripped from the journal, which lay open just an inch away. I squatted down and slid it into the light of the sun filtering through my uncovered windows.

COME FIND ME.

• • •

When I turned to look back at the house through the trees, my eyes locked onto her bedroom window. The screen was pushed out, dangling and letting in the cold. I could imagine her sticking one foot out, and then the other, lowering herself to the ground with some miraculous amount of upper-body strength. She had done it twice before, each time returned to our doorstep by a friendly neighbor, but always vowing that one day she would be gone for good. I never doubted her, and only hoped she would take me with her. This was my chance. Out of the garage door, around the house, past her broken window, under the back porch, over the river, and into the wet woods. It was easy to get lost.

It seemed like the sun went down the second I went in. Which way was the house? I calmly willed the branches to part for me, but they mocked me for thinking I was in control. How did my sister do this again and again? I looked up and saw a bluebird perched on a branch right above my head. It looked at me curiously like I didn't belong. I shooed it, and it disappeared into the clouds. I cupped my ears to listen to the sounds around me. Every time a leaf rustled in the distance, I sprung to action, even though my sister always said that no animals would harm you if you were nice to them. I could never fight a bear, anyway. It would grab me by my backpack and swing me around like a Raggedy Ann doll. It would rip up my books and eat my granola bars and call its cubs over to laugh at me.

And then I heard her calling my name. The shouts came faintly at first but then sliced through the brush to reach my ears. I stood up and tried to figure out which direction they were coming from, but the sounds just surrounded me. I tried to call back, but my voice came out tiny and raspy, having suffered from the chill. I started running.

I ran toward the first thing that looked familiar: a dilapidated gazebo we had claimed as our castle. I kept running faster and faster until I saw a purple coat emerging through the green. It was my big sister, leaning against one of the vine-covered columns. I jumped up and down and straight into her arms. She squeezed me back and brushed the crushed leaves off my hood and shoulders.

"I found you!" I screamed, trying to catch my breath. "I've been wandering around forever."

She had a backpack on one shoulder, a duffle bag on the other, and a glimmer in her eye. "It's only eight, dummy. But not a moment too soon. I have a plan." She had a sly grin on her face. "We can go anywhere we want now. We can be anything. We can go to New York City and see the biggest Christmas tree in the world!"

"How big is it?"

"It's like a hundred feet tall!"

"Okay," I said softly. "But maybe we should go home just for tonight, and we can leave in the morning?"

She looked at me like she didn't know me. "That's not our home. You know how I know?" She took off her backpack and unzipped the front pocket, beckoning me to lean in. "Look at this. I found wads of cash behind that huge portrait of their *real* son. Haven't you ever wondered why they haven't hung any pictures of *us*? They only care about him. Their flesh and blood. So this is like, a consolation prize."

"Consolation?"

"Yeah. We deserve this money. It's our ticket out of here. And check this out," she continued as she unzipped the duffle bag too. "A rabbit, like we always wanted!" She picked him up carefully and pushed him into my small arms. He was warm, and I could feel his rapid heartbeat pounding through me.

"What's his name?" I asked her through my eyelashes.

"Whatever you want it to be. This is our family, our real family. You, me, and this little dude. If we're all together, we're home." With this, she hoisted her bags back onto her back, put my backpack on her front, and grabbed my hand. We set off, the rabbit securely inside my coat, peeking out so he could watch the adventure too.

BIRACIAL IDENTITY

by

DEIDRA SUWANEE DEAS

I looked into the mirror today, smiling for a change, wondering what it would reveal. I noticed the ripples in the bronze-colored wrinkles beside my eyes, delineating the signs of wisdom that only age can bring. As I work on my Master's degree at Ivy League Cornell in Ithaca, New York, it is 1998, and the mirror conveys to me I will turn a year older this season. It is a reminder that I have traveled a long way from the reluctant womb that was a receptacle for my entrance into the South; the reluctant womb that turned away from me because I was a biracial birth following painful years of childhood neglect that ended in abandonment. Because I did not have a fit mother as many other Muscogee children had in our rural community of Uriah, Alabama, I've been coerced to find things out on my own that I otherwise would have known. I find myself realizing I've spent all my life doing this . . . and wondering if I'll spend however long I have left doing the same thing. How beneficial it would have been had I been taught the necessary life skills that come from a proper Southern woman, skills I've had to scratch and claw for—by humiliating trial and error—struggling and fighting every step of the way; indeed, fighting at times against the womb that bore me.

Anticipating an answer from the mirror, I asked, "How can I comprehend this all?" If I die like my vanilla-skinned Selena in a deadly auto-train accident, or if I die like my chocolate-skinned daddy in a tragic head-on truck collision, what will be the moral of my story? That I scratched and clawed for nothing? That my bronze-skinned life was worthless and *good for nothing* like the biological one who bore me used to say?

While these are plausible considerations, the mirror reveals there is a force inside me—a strong life force—that compels me forward and even fancies at times bronze images of *being somebody;* images of me rising above what Southerners see as unattractive mixed-race skin. The mirror shows me reflections of greatness which I have relegated to a cry for significance from my inner clay-stained child, the one who was neglected, abused and rejected; the one who, because of this, can never be whole. I have become strong—my bronze skin taut—by learning to live with the ever-present anguish of not being whole, while whole people have passed me by, enjoying their wholeness, unaware of my fragment.

SOUTHERN CHURCH

by
DEIDRA SUWANEE DEAS

There were only a few people of color at our small southern church in the Alabama Bible belt, my Muscogee family and a Latino family. Our family unconsciously blended in with whites, without knowing we were not supposed to.

All week, we worked hard, me and my siblings helping daddy with his job as janitor after school by sweeping classrooms, cleaning toilets, taking out garbage; then going to the farm to chop cotton, hoe cotton, grind corn for the cows. Sunday was the only day we got a reprieve from hard labor, got to shed dirty work clothes, and dress up for a day.

I remember that Daddy was a respected deacon at our church where he served as an usher, accountant, and greeter who handed out the church bulletins when people walked into the vestibule. He counted the offering in the offering plates that were passed around during church at the morning and evening services every Sunday. He said the money was collected for God. He often was called upon by the preacher to pray before the offering was collected, thanking God for the money they were about to receive.

In my childhood mind, I wondered how they got the money from the offering plates to God, who was unseen somewhere up in the smoke from our home fires that carried our prayers to the heavens. How *did* God get the money?

While the preacher expounded his sermon, we five children sat well behaved in the church pew, waiting for daddy to rejoin us after he finished counting the money. As the preacher advanced himself closer to the congregation by leaning over the pulpit and speaking pointed words about God, my mind wondered, and I imagined daddy put the money all together in one offering plate after he counted it and carried it up on the roof of the church. I imagined coins, wadded up dollars, paper money all lying bare in the open offering plate. I thought how a gentle breeze high up on the rooftop might blow the dollars slightly, making them shift around a little bit in the offering plate, waiting for God to come get his money. I reckoned that God, at some point, must come and take the money from the offering plate because the plates always started out empty the subsequent Sunday.

I grew a little older, and the procedures at our church changed. As respected clergy, Daddy was asked not only to count the money, but to take the offering from the Sunday services to the bank. After the evening church service, we piled into his old pickup truck that had a hard time running, and we rode with Daddy as he drove us to the bank to deposit the money that had been placed inside a white letter-sized envelope for the bank depository.

Under the dimly lit awning on the side of the bank, barren parking lot except our family, we children asked daddy if we could place the envelope into the night depository. Daddy told us, if we would take turns, he would let us put the envelope into the slot. When it was my week, I pushed the envelope filled with money into the slot, feeling exceptionally gratified to deposit the money for God. Ellanae put the enveloped money into the slot for her week, then Nadine, then Lori, then Charlie. Then it was my turn again.

Several times, the envelope was almost too fat to fit into the slot. Daddy had to help push it, wedge it, wiggle it through the slot to make it go in, remarking contentedly, "God got a lot more money in the offering plates today."

As we continued with each Sunday night deposit, I thought back on my rooftop impressions of how they placed the offering plate on the church roof. With each deposit, I came to understand my thinking had been wrong. So that's why I finally realized how God got his money. *He got it from the bank.*

ROBERTA
AND
HER COW

by

DEIDRA SUWANEE DEAS

"Yeah, we was in the woods a lot of times. Back then the cows kept the undergrowth cut down. We'd turn out the cows to pen up hogs to clean out the hogs. The next day we'd have to go way across them woods to find those cows and bring them back home.

"My mama gave me a setting hen. I took care of her and raised her. I named her Anna. I was just a little girl. She got grown and she set, and she had several little biddies. My brother Mal had some cows, and this Jersey cow got sick. He come over there—*he always wanted the cream of the crop.* He said to mama, 'I want that ole hen with those biddies. I got that ole heifer out there. You can have her, but you have to doctor her up.'

"Mama said, 'Mal, she ain't mine. She belongs to Bert.' He said, 'Well, Bert belongs to you, don't she?'

"Mama said, 'You let him have her because you know how he is. When we doctor the calf and when we get her well, you can have her.' That kinda satisfied me a little bit.

"We doctored that ole cow and doctored her. She had hollow horns and a hollow tail. We cut them horns off and filled up what was left with runtar, turpentine… We just made up a solution. Then we tied it up so she couldn't get it off. Then the tail was split and cut, and we filled it up with the solution. We got a piece of material and *wrapped it, wrapped it, wrapped it.* In a few days, the ole cow was really improved. I named her Singy. She got up and got grown.

"We always would have to turn the cows out to go to the woods to feed. And she was the leader of the bunch. She didn't get very big. My mama would get out on the back porch and she'd call, *'Cooooh, Singy!'* Singy raised her head up and listened. The next time she hears that holler, she strikes out coming this-a-way and the others would follow. She was trained pretty good.

"She was the best milk cow. I remember she gave the best milk we ever had. You could sit in a chair and milk her, and she wouldn't never move. She brought us a lot of calves. We kept her all her life. I'm always bad about doing that anyway—keeping animals around. I got a old cow out there now—the only one I got—Singy's granddaughter. My son said, 'Mama, why don't we carry old Dolly to the sale pen.' I said, '*No sir!* Dolly ain't the first the first cow and she ain't gone be the last one to die on this hill.'

"Singy's passed on. Mal's passed on. I don't know what ever become of Anna and her biddies. Singy sure lived a long time. When she died, we buried her under that oak tree over yonder. He never knowed it, but I think I got the better end of the deal than Mal."

———

THE KID
WITH THE
LONGEST BRAID

———

by
JESSICA DOE

"Beyond the cracked sidewalk and the telephone pole with layers of flyers in a rainbow of colors and the patch of dry brown grass, there stood a ten-foot high concrete block wall, caked with dozens of coats of paint. There was a small shrine at the foot of it, with burnt out candles and dead flowers and a few soggy teddy bears. One word of graffiti filled the wall, red letters on a gold background: Rejoice!"

The pop thundered through the classroom. Her eyes shot towards the rows of students—as always, it was an ocean of blank faces.

She clutched the newspaper against her chest. "Who's got gum?" she asked. Even she could hear the fatigue in her voice. *How many times have I asked this?* She thought she saw three students swallow dramatically but couldn't be certain. Nobody. Nobody was going to confess. Two weeks in the tribal school and she was still searching for some kind of grounding. "Okay," she cleared her throat. "Now, *rejoice.* Who knows what that means?" Nothing. Endless black eyes. She tucked her hair behind her ears and pulled out the tattered dictionary from her wobbly desk. "Rejoice: Feel or show great joy or delight," she read theatrically. "Cause joy to."

"Joy?" said the kid in the back row, a guttural scoff building in his throat. *What was his name?* She couldn't remember. In her mind he was The Kid with the Longest Braid. It seemed like it was taking forever to memorize names. She ran through the roster of thirty kids in her head and could see his handwriting clearly from the assignments she'd graded but couldn't come up with a name. "What they got to be joy-ful about?" he countered. "Why didn't nobody clean up those dead flowers and baby toys? Who's given dyin' things, *flowers,* to her anyway? I mean, she got killed three years ago—"

"Enough," she said as she smacked the newspaper onto the desk. "It's the anniversary of her . . . death . . . and that's not what we're supposed to be discussing with this article anyway. The purpose, if you recall, is to compare how an op-ed piece is different than—"

"I heard she got flattened so fast her shoes came clean off," Irma piped up from somewhere in back. She wriggled in her seat with dark eyes darting around the room, ready for a fight.

Before she could reply, diffuse the situation, The Kid with the Longest Braid whirled around in his seat. "I'mma whoop your ass—"

"Stop," she said as firmly as she could. It took everything in her not to slouch down into the cracked vinyl seat and rest her head on the desk like over half the students had been doing all day. "It doesn't matter . . . that's not what we're talking . . . nevermind. Now, I made everyone photocopies of this opinion piece." *With my own money,* she thought with a touch of bitterness she'd never known in herself until she'd arrived here. *Snap out of it,* she scolded herself. *You're the one who wanted this.* "As we discussed earlier, we're going to spend the Quiet Hour writing our response to the article. If you have any questions on the details, refer to the board. Again, it's between 250 and 300 words regardless of how big you write or how many pages you fill. And handwriting *will* count for part of your grade, so don't try writing excessively largely. That's the first trick they teach teachers," she offered a smile at the class, a lightening with a joke, but there were no takers. "Now, you'll be writing a personal response to this op-ed article, so it can be anything you like. Remember, this is for your creative writing credit so there's some wiggle room, but please do pay attention to the grammar we've been studying. Remember, a passive voice—"

"I won't do it," The Kid with the Longest Braid said simply. For emphasis, he shoved his notebook as far across the little desk as possible and crossed his thin arms over his chest.

She sighed. "I don't have time for this. What do you mean you're not going to do it? Everyone, pencils out. You have five minutes to re-read the article *quietly* to yourselves before we start. If you want to use the pencil sharpener, it's one at a time, one row at a time." She could have given the spiel half-asleep, and it wasn't even October yet. She still caught some jostling of students to get out of their seats first in the front row from the corner of her eye.

"What, you don't hear too good? I said I'm not gonna do it." The Kid wasn't budging, and his pencil remained unmoved on his desk. She sized him up, just ten years old, but with a knowing in his eyes of a man. For the first time in her teaching career, a fifth grader scared her. Miss Washington pulled herself up to her full height, activated her axial length like they were always talking about in yoga class, and took a shaky breath.

"You either open that notebook right now, or you're going to the principal's office." He didn't break their eye contact, still as the moment between hunter and prey. *Please open the goddamned notebook,* she willed. The principal's office was an empty threat, and she wasn't sure if the kids knew that. The principal was never there. And when she was, the last thing she had time for was babysitting a moody student.

"So do it. I don't care," The Kid said. He eased back in his seat and eyed her. A challenge.

She realized she'd been holding that deep breath and her lungs began to ache. It came out in a rush. "*Shit,* now look here—"

"Ooohh!" the kids said en masse as the forbidden four-letter word slipped out of her mouth. "Miss Washington said a bad word! She—"

"*Enough,*" she shouted to the class. Immediately silence settled over everyone. It was the first time she'd ever raised her voice in the classroom. The first time she'd raised her voice in any classroom. "Get up, you're coming with me." She took a step towards The Kid and prayed that he'd get up. All those hours of being told over and over how you *never* put a hand on a student, all the horror stories of the consequences, began to flood through her. Did those rules apply at a tribal school? On Indian land? She didn't know. She knew they had their own police department, laws, everything. *Can I lift him by the elbow without going to jail?* Surprisingly, he got up easily as she approached, but there was something different about him. His shoulders didn't slouch forward like usual and his eyes still held hers, tight, almost like a lover. Miss Washington had never had a real conversation, one on one, with him but that wasn't that unusual. His dad had shown up for the one parent-teacher conference to start the year, but as per the school's requirements the students stayed home. *Wait, the dad had shown up, right? This kid was the one whose mother wasn't there, wasn't he?* Now she couldn't remember. He faced her coolly. All she could read in him was darkness. "Forget the principal's office," she hissed. "I'm not about to bother her with this." She grabbed his notebook, copy of the article, and chewed-up pencil. Side by side, they began to march towards the back of the room like well-trained soldiers. "You'll go sit in the cubby room and write this fu—freaking paper if it takes you all day."

He stopped so quickly she was two strides ahead of him before she realized. "And what if I don't?"

Miss Washington turned slowly. The tension in the room was palpable. She could feel dozens of eyes on the two of them, little faces hungry for drama to re-tell during break. "You will. Or you'll stay there until you do."

"You think that scares me? You think keepin' me here is a threat? You have no idea, do you?"

Before she could think, before she could doubt herself, she reached towards him and grabbed his arm. It wasn't until she'd hurled him into the huge cubby closet where jackets and sack lunches were stored that she realized he was still a child. His weight in her grip shocked her. It was like releasing a bird. "Just get in there," she said as she pressed his materials firmly against his chest. She shut the heavy wooden door slowly, each creak of the rusted hinges begging her to slam it. Somehow she resisted. "What are you staring at?" she asked the class without looking at any of them. "Get to work."

When the final bell of the day rang, she let the students rush to the cubby closet and release him. Miss Washington tried not to look, not to see, and kept her head bowed over her desk as she pretended to grade papers. There was chattering and the rustling of jackets to help drown out her thoughts. They filed out in a mad group, caught only by her peripherals. She didn't know if The Kid was among the first or last to powerwalk out of the classroom and into the dusty autumn afternoon. What she did know is that throughout the rest of the day following The Incident, four long hours, there were no sounds from the cubby room. Not once did he emerge with a shy hand up motioning towards the bathroom. At recess, she stared at that proudly shut door and almost, *almost,* got up to check on him. But she didn't. The volunteer recess staff filed her class in and out for their fifteen-minutes on the dried-up grass and didn't even notice that one was missing. *Thank God this all happened after lunch,* she thought. Miss Washington didn't know if it was pride, anger, or some kind of feral-ness inside her but she wasn't certain she would have been able to let him out even to eat.

When she was certain all the students were gone and the scuffs and squeaks on the linoleum in the hallway faded to silence, she stood up. It was the longest walk across her classroom she'd ever taken, longer even than her very first day at this foreign school that seemed a throwback to the '80s. The cubby room door had been left slung open, and she could see the long-forgotten moth-eaten hoodie hanging from a plastic hanger. It had been there since the start of the school year two weeks ago, and likely for years before that. Part of her thought she'd still see him in there, stubborn and ready to fight. But there was nobody. He was gone. Sitting squarely on the low empty shelf where students put their snow boots in the winter was his notebook. The copy of the article was gone. Miss Washington sat down on the dirty shelf, not caring that the dust and grime would stain her yellow pencil skirt. She opened the notebook to nothing. Nothing. Page after page of nothing. "Goddamnit," she said under her breath. As she flipped towards the center, the crisp empty pages gave way to drawings. Profiles of a middle-aged woman crafted with such skill and detail she briefly wondered if someone else had done it. But something in her marrow told her this was all him. The profiles of the woman gave way to incredibly detailed sketchings of a little girl with twin braids. She looked mildly familiar, but then again there was a preschool connected to the tribal school and it could easily be one of the many toddlers and little ones she nearly tripped over every day getting to the classroom. He'd filled dozens of pages with intricate portraits of the little girl, occasionally punctuated with images of the woman. She couldn't tell how old the sketches were, but it must have taken him weeks, months, if not years to complete this kind of expansive portfolio. She let out a sigh as she slowly flipped towards the end of the notebook. Just as she was about to close it, just as her heart softened for The Kid, she turned to the last page. It was filled with his neat handwriting, a slanted cursive that leaned so heavily to the right the words looked close to toppling over.

Rejoyse? Re-joy? There wasn't no joy in the 1ˢᵗ place All these jornalis actin like Mimis death spot is some kind of memoryal is stupid They dumb or somthing???? Dont they get taut better than that in collage??? The stupid ass holes who rote that on Mimis spot dont no anything about nothing + she HATED teddybears She said they were scary and thot theyd come alive at nigt Dont the jornalis now that??? and all thos flowers are dum to Why are peple leving stuff thats gonna die that dosnt make sense If they realy want to give stuff to Mimi they shuld give stuff she like d like spong bob or that powerpuf stuff Evry one is talking abot the wall and all the ~~pant~~ *PAINT like its som kinda secret and thats dum to I can tell no NDN rote this OPED thing or whatevr EVRYONE nos why Mimi colord that wall difrent colors You all stupid???? Thats* ~~her~~*Wher R mama was killd + now Mimi killd ther to and mama got raypt + left ther + all thos peple riting badshit abot mama mayd Mimi mad I was mad to but Mimi brav E enuff to do somthing Mimi p a int over all the bad stuff evry time No body gonna call mama a hor or slut + If id ben with Mimi that day I dont think she wud got killd cuz with 2 of us that car wud saw us She was to litle but lots bravr then me But im gonna do what i shudda don b4 im gonna make it rite i dont no how many words this is but thats all THE END*

"My God," she whispered as she let the notebook fall shut in her lap. Miss Washington stood and took deliberate steps back to her desk, her heels clicking like gunfire. She pulled out the bright violet stack of Post-It notes, brand-new and bought from her own funds at the start of the year. *A,* she wrote boldly with her new bronze Sharpie pen. When she'd started teaching, she swore she'd never use red. It was too aggressive and nobody wanted to try to resuscitate a dying paper. Black was just too somber. Now, she wished for somber. For something suitable for a funeral. Looking at the naked "A", she added a plus sign. *Come talk to me,* she added in her scrawled handwriting. It wasn't enough and reeked of an afterthought, but it was all she could offer. She placed the notebook on The Kid's desk, stood back, then straightened it so it was aligned perfectly in the center.

It took her two hours to get ready the next morning. Ninety minutes of which involved simply pulling herself out of bed. There was a dread settled in her throat heavy as an autumn nesting bird. She came up with score of excuses not to go into the classroom. It's not like it would be an anomaly at the school anyway. They'd jumped at the chance to hire her, even though the only indigenous blood she could claim was a grandfather who said he had some kind of Cherokee in him, and even she knew everyone said that. But she had a teaching degree from one of the Ivy League schools most people forgot about and the kind of youthful energy school administrators thought could handle these kids. As she slipped into the cool seat of her little coupe, something else took the wheel. She didn't know how or why, but instead of her usual route along smooth paved roads, she took the side streets that snaked towards that fall-apart memorial. She rounded the corner and saw a gathering of people, all ages, from babies cradled in parents' arms to elders with their hand-carved canes. They looked like disciples, tired and weary at the end of their pilgrimage. Disciples or a riot in the making. She couldn't make out where they were all coming from. In seconds it had grown from a dozen people to twenty. Thirty. She was surrounded. Miss Washington slowed to a crawl as she approached, forced into stillness by the mob. *This isn't normal. Is it?* she wondered. The crowd shifted slightly and she could make out a milk crate at the base of the painted wall, right in the center. The Kid was unmistakable, his braid shining in the morning light. He carried a bullhorn in his hand, held together with duct tape. But draped in regalia, the bullhorn suddenly looked like Excalibur. The car came to a stop, engulfed by people who easily stepped around the freshly waxed vehicle. She pulled up the emergency brake and stepped into the mist. Arms folded in like wings, she wove her way through the crowd toward him.

The Kid got up onto a milk crate and raised his hand. A murmur went through the crowd and then it fell silent, except for a few people shouting words of encouragement at him. The Kid acknowledged them with a nod and a shy smile. In the full light of day, he looked less angry and more beautiful. He waited until people stopped shouting. A siren could be heard, maybe five or ten blocks away. The Kid raised the bullhorn, pressed the button, and began to speak.

• • •

His heart thundered in his chest and though it felt like his hands were shaking, when he looked down they were still. *Myocardium,* he thought to himself. *Be quiet.* In the brigade of faces, some were familiar but he couldn't think of names. Either his father hadn't heard about the rally, which was doubtful given how fast words spread, or he'd chosen not to come. It didn't matter either way. As he lifted the bullhorn to his lips, there were no words prepared. He simply trusted that what needed to be said would come forth.

"My mama was killed here five years ago," he said. Silence washed across the crowd. Never before had he held such command. It fueled him, and for once he felt heard. "My sister, Mimi, two years later. I . . ." He felt tears begin to sting in his eyes. *Shit, I thought I was over all this.* He glanced down and was taken by a pair of clear blue eyes, alien in the crowd. Miss Washington gazed up at him, the only white person in the crowd. At the sight of her, even with the anger from yesterday rinsed out of those blue eyes, he felt a rage start to build in his center. It overrode the sadness. "I didn't wanna believe it. When they told me," he said. "And they never caught the guy that, you know, with my mama. But that don't mean anything because I know. We all know," he continued. "It doesn't matter a *damn* who it was. Because this is what I know for sure: It wasn't any of us. Mama, she was working in the city the night she never came home. She was *dumped* here, police know that."

As if on cue, the sirens finally arrived. He saw the rez police trucks sidle up to the outskirts of the crowd. Faces he'd known his whole life in their tan baseball caps and shiny badges began to approach. One mumbled something incoherent into his walkie talkie. "Go on, son," one of the elders urged from just left of the *Rejoice's* R.

"We know this—my mama wasn't raped on this land. Wasn't murdered here either, at least it didn't start here. My guess, it was a setup. A *sloppy* setup. Come dump her body on the rez, and nobody'd look nowhere because the secrets kept here aren't like nothing I've seen before."

"Get down," one of the officers yelled gruffly from the sidelines. "Or we'll help ya with it."

"Leave him alone, that little boy—" Miss Washington rushed at the police, but he just tipped his head back and laughed. The Kid watched as she faltered, uncertain.

"I don't need no white savior," The Kid bellowed into the bullhorn. "Especially not you."

"And she don't have any power to be saving anybody anyhow," the officer added. "Now, get down, boy. You're riling everyone up."

"That's the point," he said firmly. "Don't—don't you think we should be riled up? I'm telling you, my mama was dumped here. My sister ran over in a hit-and-run by a coupla drunks, and all because *someone* or some people were writing that shit on this, I don't know, this some kinda grave. *Shouldn't we be "riled up"?*

"Kid's got a point," the elder said with a slow nod. "Wasn't like this before. And that trash that kept getting' written here—"

"Investigation's ongoing," the cop said with a shrug. "We're not inviting any kind of vigilante justice here. Why don't all you folks go on home, and *you*," he said pointedly to the boy. "Shouldn't you be in school?"

The boy choked down a laugh. "School? This is insane . . ."

The walkie talkie rambled something that couldn't be made out. "C'mon then, boy," the cop said as he pushed through the crowd. "You're comin' with me."

"No," he said. He pressed the bullhorn closer to his lips. "And there's nothing you can do about it. I'm not doing anything wrong. None of us here are doing anything wrong. You're the one s'posed to fix this. When are you gonna fix all this? This is *your* fault—"

"Don't think I won't beat your ass like your daddy shoulda." The cop leaned closer, nearly nose to nose thanks to the quivering milk crate beneath the boy's feet. "Maybe if there'd been more discipline at home, your mama and little sister of yours would still be alive."

The boy felt the bullhorn drop from his fingers but never heard it hit the ground. A cool licking began at his elbows. Even through the buckskin, he could feel the rhythm. The crowd merged into one, a living, breathing single entity. "Oh, my God," he heard a voice say. Miss Washington's. He didn't know where the cop's face went or why he was suddenly somehow facing the wall. The letters were so big, so vibrant, that all he saw was red. REJOICE was gone, or maybe he was inside it. He didn't know, all he knew is that there was a fire within him that burned something fierce yet wrapped him in comfort. It felt like his mama's arms, the squeeze of his sister's small hand, his grandmother's paper-thin hands on his cheeks.

". . . the hell is that . . ." a voice broke through his basking, but just barely. The question poked at the perimeter of his being, an annoyance he easily pushed away. He was weightless, a feather. There was no more creaking milk crate beneath his feet, but somehow he was solid. He was held.

"Snake," he heard a voice shout somewhere in the distance. It was far away, stretches away. The voice was afraid, but he wasn't, even as he felt the slithering make its way from the small of his back up his spine and stretch across his shoulder blades. His wings that had been waiting to be birthed.

• • •

Nobody talked about it, that was the strangest part. Miss Washington could pack everything she'd brought into the classroom in just two canvas totes. It wasn't in the local news, and it seemed nobody off the reservation had been there—besides her. But when she gave her notice to the principal, the big-bellied woman just shrugged and pushed paperwork towards her. "You, I mean . . . the school has substitutes, right?" The principal just shrugged again, and Miss Washington couldn't tell if it was a positive or negative gesture.

Her mother had sighed deeply when she'd called her to say she was leaving. "Didn't I tell you?" she asked. "You're better than that, running off to 'do good' at some poor school with those *Indians,* you're an *Ivy League college-educated woman.* What were you thinking?"

"I don't . . . I'm sorry," she'd muttered into the phone. What was she supposed to say? That one of her students' braids had turned into a snake and he'd glided towards the heavens?

There was no way she was going to stay, not after what had happened. When The Kid's braid began to hiss and S-curve up his back, she'd stumbled backward in fear. The cop was the only one who followed suit. The others pushed closer while still keeping a respectable distance. It's like they'd seen it before, and maybe they had. And she could have sworn The Kid's feet weren't touching the crate. He was floating, eyes closed and face cast upward.

She had wondered at who shrieked "Snake!" so close to hear it almost burst her ear drum until the young woman next to her gently grasped her forearm.

"That's not a snake like you think," the woman said quietly, a closed-lipped smile on her face. Then she said another name, one with ancient roots that wouldn't fit in Miss Washington's mouth. "You know what this is, don't you?" the woman asked her without taking her eyes of The Kid. "This is a blessin'. You're witnessing a blessing from the ancestors. From Creator."

Miss Washington had barreled through the crowd to her car, not daring to look back. The Kid had drawn everyone so close that there were no more human obstacles to weave her little coupe around. For a moment she thought the engine wouldn't start, just like in a horror movie, because what else could this be? But it purred to life with ease. As she'd pulled away, she risked one look into her rearview mirror and wondered at her sanity. *Am I imagining all of this?* The crowd had fallen to their knees, and the cop was nowhere to be seen. The Kid floated, there was no denying it, his head nearly reaching the top of that high painted wall. So high that REJOICE was displayed like a promise at his feet.

A note on the story: The number of murdered and missing indigenous women (MMIW) in the US and Canada has reached epidemic proportions. While there is no comprehensive data in the US, as an example, indigenous people make up two percent of all people in Washington state but five percent of missing persons. The majority are women and girls. As a member of the Cherokee Nation, much of my work focuses on Native American disparities and creating narratives that can help bring these discussions to light. While "The Kid with the Longest Braid" is obviously a work of fiction, it addresses very real issues and utilizes a wide range of symbolisms that pay homage to this systemic trend of violence and oppression within indigenous communities (i.e. the only named characters are female and Mama, Mia, Irma and [Miss] Washington, an acronym for MMIW; the symbolism of snakes within many Native tribes for re-birth, etc., the paradox of The Kid threatening Irma with violence while simultaneously wanting to protect his mama and sister, etc.).

THE AXE

by
MARK ENNIS

The border between the United States and Canada existed to some people but not to my father. He called it an illusion created by men with broken minds. I never saw much of a border either way, other than an occasional old fenceline broken in places, with a sign saying "Entering Canada" or "Entering the United States of America."

It was mid-November, and the snow had already fallen and covered everything. It was a beautiful and sad time of year. I knew things still grew in the winter, but what you saw, what you felt, was death. We were always ready, though. My mother was a good cook. She made sure we were well fed with her store of provisions and canned goods. My father was good with a gun, and so we had enough meat.

My father usually didn't worry about these things, but this year he was concerned about having enough wood for the cabin. In the past year the local logging companies had cut down most of the white ash trees in Northern Maine. "They burn the best," he'd always say. For some reason he didn't touch the trees on the reserve.

He was good with an axe too. He had a real nice one with a long ash handle and blade sharper than a pit of thorns. He kept it sharp, since he used it so much. And was it ever heavy.

The logging companies always hired him. They thought he was some kind of magician with that axe. He'd put down a tree faster than the strongest of the white cutters. He thought nothing of it, but they sure did. Since he got paid per tree, he got paid better than them. Well, one day a few months back some of those white men told the site manager that my father had to go or they would "use that goddamn axe to chop off his head." At least that's the way he heard it around the logging camp. So they made up some reason or other to fire him. He received a letter of reference from the company as a gesture of goodwill. He said it didn't matter much, though. Other than the logging camp, there weren't many jobs for Indians good with an axe.

I'm not sure how my mother felt about it, but it was nice to have him around the house. He started patching things up, fixing things here and there. He also spent a lot of time in the woods, going for walks, collecting scrap wood. I liked to tag along when he went on these walks, especially when he went out chopping. I couldn't do much myself being so small other than pile the split pieces on our sled.

On one occasion, he was working through a fallen pine tree. He had a good sweat going even with the cold. He suddenly stopped and looked around.

"It'll be a long cold winter. Colder than the last. We'll have to be ready."

When I asked him why we'd need to be ready, he remained silent. Then he just said he would try even harder this year to protect us. The words didn't surprise me, but the way he said them did. They sounded uncertain and full of fear. As we were going home, I noticed how silent the trees were without their leaves.

During supper that night, my mother told him to keep his axe in the shed where it belonged. She was always after him, giving him a hard time for this or that. He didn't mean anything by it, bringing it inside like that. I just think he felt stronger with it near him. She treated me pretty cold too. He said she was the only thing colder than a Maine winter. That gave me a good laugh. I used to think that all the firewood he brought in the house was just to warm her up.

My mother had a pious streak, but it never made any sense to me. She sort of used religion like a weapon. She'd go on about "God this," "Jesus that," or "That's the devil making you do that," and so on.

All that pestering made me start hating God. I was scared of thinking that way since she said God knew everything, even stuff in your head, but I figured that since I wasn't in Hell . . . yet . . . maybe he just took a liking to me or overlooked me entirely. God was white, and white people seemed to mostly ignore Indians down here on earth.

One afternoon in the shed before winter came, I was set to ask my father about all this fussing she made over God. I knew his feelings on the subject. He told me once that God was perfectly fine for those that believed in such things. I was watching him build a new table for the kitchen out of a bunch of wood scraps he collected. I enjoyed watching him work. The smell of pine filled the shed, and the open door showcased the brilliant hues of autumn. I must have let on that something was troubling me. He sensed such things.

"You have something you want to ask, don't you?"

"Yes. But maybe I shouldn't."

He kept eyeing his level. "It's about your mother, isn't it?"

I was just getting my nerve up when I heard a horse braying suddenly. I went to the open door. The serene autumnal backdrop now included Jim Jenkins on a beautiful chestnut brown horse. Jenkins was an Indian Agent, a man employed by the US government to bring law and order and peace to the reserve. I found out quick that he wasn't very good at his job.

He began dismounting the horse. My father joined me at the door, looking out at Jenkins just as his freshly oiled black boots hit the ground.

"Wait here."

My father's body changed as he approached him. It was only about thirty feet to the front of our cabin but along the way my father's normal, forceful stride was replaced with a subtle, withdrawn and withered kind of walk. He seemed to hesitate with each step forward.

I sized them both up once my father reached him. They stood eye to eye. Neither seemed physically stronger than the other. The main difference was the state of their clothes. Jenkins' clothes were fresh and clean, while my father's were worn in, having accrued the earth's dust over time. That didn't surprise me. I knew we were poor. My mother always reminded us of that fact. There was a light breeze that carried the conversation to my ears.

"I swear you Indians think you're owed everything under the sun. I'm here to tell you that ain't so."

Jenkins spoke with a violent kind of eloquence, the edges of his voice full of tension. My father said nothing. The wind suddenly carried the silence. He looked over and saw me watching. Jenkins also looked at me then turned back to my father.

"Last week, were you hunting quail off-reserve, and don't lie about it."

He didn't have his axe, but he didn't need it. I waited anxiously for him to tell Jenkins to go to hell.

"What concern is it of yours?"

"It's not what concerns me. If I'm bringing it to your attention, it concerns you. That's the end of it. So. Did you go off hunting where you weren't supposed to?"

He remained silent.

"Answer me, Goddammit!"

The horse stirred at his outburst. My father nodded subtly.

"How many times do we have to go through this. You don't do anything without my say-so."

"There's nothing left to hunt on the reserve."

"Yes, there is. You're either too lazy or just a lousy hunter."

Jenkins mounted the horse, suddenly looking enormous. On the ground, they were even but now my father was looking up to him. I can see he did so reluctantly.

"My patience has run out. You keep taking advantage of my goodwill, but that stops today. And that white wife of yours won't make me confer any more of it. She chose to marry you."

He pressed his legs into the horse's side and began going back the way he came, the dark woods quickly absorbing him. My father came back into the shed. I was embarrassed for him, and he knew it. I forgot the question I meant to ask. It was for the best. Some things were better off not knowing.

After a few weeks he started getting restless. My mother was hounding him about money, and truth be told, even I was getting worried. We were low on provisions and our store of meat. I think Jenkins somehow got into my father's head.

The weather turned in early December, each day's grey-coated sky a cold reminder of a hard winter to come. It wasn't long before a blizzard came. I was in a good mood the day it hit. The teachers loved wailing on the Indian kids at school, but I made it through the whole day without any of them hitting me. My mother was cutting up vegetables for a stew when I got home. The cabin was very cold, so I knew she was rationing wood.

"Hello, Ma."

She barely smiled. She didn't show much in the way of love, which you probably gathered by now. My father said she showed it by cooking and tending to my needs. I suppose he was right. It still didn't feel like it was enough.

I put my tin lunch pail down on the new kitchen table. I saw some old dusty black and white photos laying on it. I picked up one of the photos and saw a smiling baby girl on her stomach. In another, I saw the same baby girl sitting on my mother's lap. They both looked so happy.

She saw me looking at the photo. She came over and quickly grabbed it from my hand. She gathered up the rest and put them in her apron pocket. I had seen one of the photos before. One night my mother fell asleep on her rocking chair reading the Bible. The photo was sticking out of Deuteronomy, so I took a peek when it fell to the floor.

Anyway, she went back to cooking, pretending nothing happened. The wind picked up and began whistling through the entire cabin. I noticed the fire in the wood stove was almost out. Near the stove, there were about four pieces of wood. I grabbed one of the pieces to put in the stove.

"You leave that wood be. I'm saving those for tonight."

I let both her and the wood be. I had a good day and her sour mood wasn't going to ruin it. I decided to go looking for my father. I put on some waders and headed out. He wasn't in the shed, but his axe was gone, so I figured he went chopping.

There was a little bit of an impression of tracks leading from the shed into the woods, so I followed them. The snow was whirling and getting all over the few uncovered parts of my body, my neck and my wrists especially.

After about twenty minutes, I heard a faint yet distinct noise, the sound of an axe piercing wood. I was near a small frozen brook. I waited and listened. The noise came from across the brook, past the remaining pieces of an old broken fence that marked the border. The "Entering Canada" sign was covered with fresh white. I stepped in the brook slowly, breaking up the newly formed ice. The water came up well above my knees, but my waders protected me for the most part. My coat got a bit wet, but I didn't mind. The cold water made me feel alive, and the winter air expanded my small lungs, making me cough. The chopping paused for a moment.

I moved towards the noise, each thwap calling me closer. I saw my father in a sweat, chopping up a fallen ash in a small clearing. He had a number of pieces cut, almost enough for half a cord of wood. He turned around when he heard my feet crunching the icy snow.

"John. What are you doing out here?"

"I came looking for you. Ma is in a terrible mood."

He put down his axe and gave me a warm smile.

"Yeah. She seems to be having a day, I guess."

I looked around. Even though the woods surrounded us, things felt different.

"Are we still on the reserve?"

"No. Once you pass that fence, you're in Canada."

"You mean we're not in Maine now?"

"That's right."

I looked around expecting something different to jump out at me, but it didn't. It looked like the rest of the bush. As a matter of fact, it always did.

"How come you didn't cut on the reserve?"

"Well, I don't recognize that fence. It doesn't mean anything to me."

I listened, but I couldn't make sense of it.

"Here. Help me load some of this wood."

We put about half of it on our sled.

"Let's head back. We'll get the rest later after we eat."

He pushed the sled through the snow and then through the border. When we got to the brook, he brushed a thick coating of snow off an eight-foot-long piece of heavy rectangular plywood near the bank. I hadn't seen it when I waded through. He picked up the plywood, carefully stood it up, and then pushed it down so that it covered the length of the brook. He slid the sled carefully on the wood "bridge," and we pushed it across.

By the time we got home, the stew was ready. My mother looked at the fresh wood once we placed it near the stove.

"Is that enough?"

"It'll do for a few days. Plus, I left half out there."

We ate a warm meal in a warm house that evening. I knew there wouldn't be any school the next day (and even if there was, I wasn't going). I got real tired, so I went to bed early. I was under the covers in my cot, reading a comic book. The warm air seeped in from the kitchen, so much so that I even kept my window open. I began drifting to sleep when my mother's voice brought me out of the first dream of the night. Her calm voice couldn't hide her worries.

"What are you trying to prove anyway? Getting this wood off-reserve. I heard what he said to you."

My father was usually quiet when confronted by my mother's many accusations and opinions, but not this time. He spoke direct but calmly to her.

"I'm not trying to prove anything. I'm tired of hiding out in the open. Jim Jenkins can rot in hell."

She let out a small, sneering laugh.

"I'm tired of living hand-to-mouth. Being an Indian is hard enough, and these Indian Agents just make it harder."

"What you did was stupid."

"I have to feed my family. Keep this cabin warm."

"Even so, you're creating a heap of trouble for us."

"I don't see it that way. The reserve is like a goddamn plantation nowadays."

I noted the word. I had never heard it before. It sounded harmless, like a place where good things grow.

"We should be out there on all the land. Not just this land . . . I'm not living like my father did. I need to be an example for John."

"He saw the photos today."

"What?"

"I had them out."

"Why would you do that?"

"Do you know what day it is?"

"Yes."

"She would've been eleven."

Eventually the voices went away, replaced by a black peace that opened up a whole night of bright dreams.

I awoke the next morning practically frozen. The open window created a constellation of icy frost on the little glass pane. I looked out the window and saw that the blizzard was over. The kitchen was empty, and the fire in the stove was completely out. The door of the cabin was wide open, too. I felt so lonely. I could see out front that everything was covered in deep white, then further into the woods, a mix of white, with bits of brown, grey, and green. I put on my winter snowsuit and cinched my boots tight.

That was when I saw my mother coming out from the woods,

white as a ghost. She appeared to float on top of the snow. When she came in, she remained silent. She sat down at the kitchen table just sort of in a daze. She then looked at me, through me more like it. I waited for her to talk, but she wouldn't.

"Where's Papa?"

"He said he'd be back right away. I heard a commotion out in the woods. It carried right to my ears."

I let her be and went looking. The blizzard must have stopped overnight since his tracks were fresh. They were easy to find, since they were much bigger than my mother's tracks.

The wind picked up, and it was still very cold. I kept going until I reached the frozen brook. The tracks continued on to the other side so I followed them, through the fence and back to where we got the wood in the clearing the day before. The snow was thick.

I found the sled with some of the leftover wood already placed on it. Nothing seemed out of sorts until I saw some blood on the snow just near the sled. I looked around and saw tracks going every which way in the clearing. It took me a few moments to find the right path. I followed it. I soon found another stain of blood under a low hanging tree branch jutting out from the woods. From there, I found a wide smooth track cutting a clear path through to the woods. It was about the width of a man. I followed it for about forty steps. Frozen blood dotted the path the whole way.

Suddenly, the smooth track ended. I looked into the woods and saw a path that seemed wide enough for a wagon, and sure enough I saw a set of wagon wheels dug into the snow. I followed them at a steady pace, and after a good hour I reached another clearing, where I saw it, a windowless little shack set in the middle of snow-covered pines.

There was no one around. I approached it slowly. The wagon tracks ended at the front of the shack. The door had a heavy, rusted metal padlock on it. The scene confounded me, a true mix of beauty and ugliness.

I walked around it a few times, taking in all the details, the color of the wood, the rotten eaves, the rusted nails pounded into the planks. I counted how many steps it took to walk around it. Just under a hundred. I saw the wagon tracks again near the front of the shack, going off into another direction back into the woods.

I tried looking inside, at least where I found tiny cracks or little holes, but I couldn't see anything, even when I squinted. The wind blew hard, yet it was somehow quiet. I remembered the silence of the trees. I felt scared, cold, and alone. I wasn't sure what to do, so I headed back home.

On the way back I passed the sled again. I saw his axe this time. I didn't see it before, but the wind had since swept away some of the snow that was covering its long handle. I picked it up and felt its weight. It was heavy, so I carried it with both hands the rest of the way home.

When I arrived, Jim Jenkins was there on his magnificent brown horse, surrounded by two other men on horses not nearly as beautiful. He was talking to my mother. I got pretty close to them. He stopped talking to look at me but then paid me no mind and went back to hectoring her. I noticed he had a badly bruised cheek. The two other men looked at my mother in an unsettling way.

"He's not one to learn. Violence begets violence."

"He was just trying to keep the cabin warm. Show some mercy!"

"I have. He's lucky I didn't shoot him dead. Especially after the cheap shot he took at me. And don't forget, if he had been caught on the other side of the border, he'd have a whole set of other troubles."

"It's not fair."

"Maybe so, but it has to be done."

"How long will he be in there?"

"Until he learns. That's how long."

"He'll freeze in there!"

"So be it."

He looked at me again, recognizing the axe in my hand.

"Now boy, don't you go and foul up like your father. You use that axe where you're told, you hear?"

I gripped the axe, noting the smooth handle from its many years of use. I wondered if it had ever been used to kill. He and the other men rode away slowly into the woods, the low winter sun now mostly obscured by the tall tree line. My mother began crying, looking lost, as she went back into the cabin.

That night at dinner, we had leftover stew with biscuits, but for all I remember I could've been eating sawdust. After dinner, I saw her put some white powder in a glass of water. Soon after she drank it, she was fast asleep in her room. I tended the fire and kept the house warm. I thought about going back out to the shack but then I had to watch her as well. I decided to go to bed. I tried reading my comic that night, but it was no use.

I left the window in my room open all day, so it was very cold. As I closed it, I could hear sleet begin to fall, the bits of ice dancing as they hit the roof and the ground until they found their eventual resting place.

I woke early the next morning. I felt different. It may have been the hate settling in. I didn't like the feeling at all. I checked on my mother, but she was still asleep. I placed my finger under her nose and felt warm air. I was grateful that she didn't throw up in her sleep like the last time she took that powder. I had trouble pushing her on her side and cleaning up that time. I never told my father about that.

I got his canteen and filled it with water. I then found some biscuits and a bit of leftover stew and put it in his lunch pail. I put the canteen in my knapsack and carried the lunch pail since it didn't fit in my knapsack. I made sure to grab my father's axe and headed out.

Ice covered the tracks from the day before, but I remembered the way. I crossed the brook, then the ice-coated fence on to the little clearing where my father had been chopping wood. The sled was gone. I kicked myself for not bringing it back home yesterday. I saw the sled tracks and some footprints going off in a different direction back into Maine. They weren't my father's tracks, so I kept on.

The cold air hammered my little lungs, and walking through the icy path caused my legs to ache. I worked up a good sweat by the time I arrived. When I reached the clearing, the sun was shining bright, the brightness even harsher with the ice reflecting the sun's rays. The shack remained the same, except it was covered in ice.

I still wasn't sure what to do, and I was still scared. The door was coated with ice. I slowly lifted the axe and hit the door softly a few times with the tip of it. It was so heavy.

"Papa? Papa, it's me."

I listened hard.

The silence in return was memorable. I walked slowly around the shack, slipping and sliding quite a bit as I looked for a place to begin my inquiry. I was once again at the door. I began lifting the axe over my head, but I slipped and fell to the ground. The heavy blade almost cut my leg. I got up and eventually found my footing. I remembered the question I meant to ask as the axe hit the ice.

BORDER CROSSING (1963)

by
JANE HAMMONS

Laurie Bow Kerchee marked the twenty-third big red X on her calendar and was just about to sit down for a good cry when the phone rang. It was the secretary of Del Valle Elementary School telling her that Annie Kay was in the Nurse's Room with a fever. Laurie set her crying time aside, got into her truck, and drove slowly down the dirt road muddy from a storm the night before, until she reached the highway that led to the school three miles away. She parked and hurried up the cement steps, poking her head into the office and waving at the secretary to let her know she had arrived to pick up her daughter.

Zibah Rascoe checked on Annie Kay Kerchee then sat down at her desk in the Nurse's Office and filled out a job application. Several months ago she had received her Master's in Nursing from the University of California Medical School. Living for two years in San Francisco had made her return to the little community of Del Valle, New Mexico, especially difficult. She missed the restaurants and shops and museums, but more than anything she missed living in a city where she could walk, have a chat with neighbors, and listen to music in nightclubs filled with people who looked like her. But her sister's recent death left her nephew to care for. Zibah loved Downey like a son, but she didn't want to get stuck in a job she could have gotten without her Master's because she now had a boy to raise. She had dreams. And she wanted him to have them, too.

Laurie knocked on the wire mesh glass of the door to Zibah's office. Through the murky distortion of the thick gray window Zibah read the distress on Laurie's face. "It's just a fever," she said, opening the door. "I gave her an aspirin about ten minutes ago."

Laurie slumped down hard into the chair next to the desk and wept. Zibah couldn't remember seeing Laurie cry more than a handful of times: when she was seven and got bucked off a horse and broke her arm; a couple of years ago when her grandmother Estelle died; and the day she was expelled from high school because she was pregnant. "What's going on? Be quick. I need to give a menstruation talk to the sixth grade girls in about ten minutes."

"We use protection. Foam. I have a diaphragm. When I can convince him to, Dan wears a rubber." Mindful of Annie Kay in the Nurse's Room across the hall, Laurie whispered all the ways she had tried to prevent the pregnancy as though she needed to earn Zibah's approval before asking, "Can you help me?"

"I can try." Zibah belonged to an underground network of nurses, activists, and a handful of nuns who found doctors in Mexico to provide safe abortions. The group she had worked with in California was larger than that in New Mexico, but she got reliable information out of El Paso. "I can't take you, though. We might attract attention. The Border Patrol keeps an eye out for women of childbearing age crossing into Juárez. A Black woman with a white woman." She shrugged off the look Laurie shot her. "I know you're Comanche and Cherokee along with white. But you can pass." She shook her head. "I don't want to get stopped. People around here are already stirred up because the school hired a Black nurse. Some of them would just love a reason to get rid of me, and sending me to jail for helping women get abortions would add an extra dose of pleasure."

"I understand," said Laurie. "I can go alone. Just tell me where. I'll get a room in El Paso and spend the night if I need to."

"That's not how it works. We follow the rules, no exceptions. If there are complications, and you have to go to a hospital, or if you get stopped at the border and look sick or are bleeding—and believe me, they can pull you over for no reason other than being a young woman—they can call a doctor to examine you and put you in jail, Laurie, on either side of the border. And the doctor and nurses, too, if they find them. You need to have someone with you who knows what to do. There are two doctors in Juárez whose facilities we've approved. They'll perform the procedure if you are not more than fourteen weeks pregnant."

"I'm not. My periods are really regular. It's how I know I'm . . ." She choked off the word *pregnant*. Laurie pounded her fists on her thighs. "I feel so stupid. I'm twenty-nine. I thought I knew how to avoid this."

"You're not stupid, Laurie." Zibah sighed. "It might take me a while to find a driver. I don't know of anyone within a hundred miles to work with. You'll probably have to drive to Las Cruces, maybe El Paso. It was easier in California, to find volunteers to drive. It's much harder here. And more dangerous. Especially for me. To be asking around." Zibah checked her watch.

Laurie stood. "I'm sorry Annie Kay is going to miss your talk. She knows about periods. That I have them and she'll get them. But I know you have so much more to tell these girls. Things she needs to know." She managed a smile before going into the room where her eleven-year-old daughter lay on a cot, her cheeks flushed, her long dark hair matted with sweat around her face. "Hey, there," she said, gently rousing her daughter with hand on her shoulder and a kiss on her forehead. "Let's go home. You got all your stuff here?"

Zibah met them at her office door with a paper cup of cold water for Annie Kay. "Drink this," she said. "And lots of fluids when you get home."

"Ginger ale?" Annie Kay asked, her eyes glassy with fever.

"Of course." Laurie pressed her daughter close and squeezed back tears.

Laurie changed the red crayon for a purple one to mark the days until Zibah called. In the seven that passed, Annie Kay recovered from the bug that had kept her home. "Are you getting sick?" Annie Kay asked Laurie on the day she went back to school. "You don't look so good."

"I'm fine." Laurie assured her daughter. "I'm just behind." She pointed to her sewing machine where the alterations she did for several clothing stores in town sat next to a pile of the ironing she took in.

"Sorry," said Annie Kay.

Laurie kissed the top of her daughter's head. "I'll get caught up real quick." She knew her daughter worried about her work. How much she had. If it was enough. She had been the same way as a child. Raised by her grandmother in the same little house where she and Annie Kay lived, Laurie and her grandmother had supported themselves by taking in laundry and delivering eggs from their chickens. They also sold their beadwork at powwows and fairs. When her grandmother got sick, Laurie stopped taking in laundry so she'd have more time to help her out. When she died, Laurie gave up the chickens and began taking in ironing and alterations. She made time for beading when she could. And if she really needed money, she sold some of her grandmother's old pieces. She rubbed the surface of the bracelet on her wrist: a turtle design beaded in orange and green. Estelle gave it to her on the day she arrived in Del Valle, shortly after her mother's death. It was a piece she'd never sell, no matter how broke.

When Laurie got back from taking Annie Kay to the bus, she heard the telephone ringing and raced to answer it.

"Next Thursday morning," said Zibah. "A driver will meet you at La Posta Restaurant in Mesilla. If there's a spot under the trees near the service entrance, park your truck there by 11:00." Zibah hesitated. She knew Laurie was sensitive about her old International Harvester panel truck. It still bore the ghost of Estelle's business— Comanche Egg and Wash. As a girl, Laurie had been ridiculed mercilessly about her Comanche eggs and her dirty Indian laundry when she made deliveries and pickups in town.

"I know it's conspicuous. I thought about borrowing Dan's for the drive, but then I have to make up a story about why I can't drive my own."

"I could switch with you for the day. But that might raise questions, too. It can't be helped. You should be able to drive it to the motel afterwards. And if not, we'll make arrangements with the driver."

"Thank you, Zi. So much."

"You'll need to take seventy-five dollars with you. I know that's a lot, but it's about half the fee. The organization picks up half the cost. I can loan you some if you need it."

"I've got it," said Laurie. Money was always a problem, but she had an emergency fund, which was also her college fund. She didn't touch it unless she had to.

"Annie Kay can stay with me and Downey."

"Thanks," said Laurie. "She's comfortable enough with Dan, but I don't think she'd want him to babysit her. And I don't know how I'd ask . . ." Laurie had been seeing Dan for a couple of years, and she didn't want to lie to him about where she was going, but she would not tell him the truth.

"They'll probably drive me crazy. I'll just let them watch TV all night." Zibah laughed. "So, you'll need to dress like a housewife. Like town women on Sundays but not too fancy. I know this sounds paranoid. But you must not attract attention."

"Everything by the book," said Laurie. "Promise." She imagined herself in different well-dressed housewife roles. Laura Petrie, Donna Reed, Samantha from *Bewitched,* but she didn't own pearls or pencil skirts or tight capris. In the pile of other women's clothes that needed to be ironed, she found a belted, front-pleat dress with a scoop neck and shirred skirt in an aqua and pale pink splash of cabbage roses, something she'd never choose for herself. She could wash and iron it when she returned. No one would know. Hair in a French twist. Pale lipstick. Respectable housewife.

On Thursday it rained, so Laurie drove Annie Kay to the end of the road and waited with her for the school bus. She reminded her to go home with Zibah and Downey after school. Once her daughter was on her way, Laurie changed into her borrowed clothes and put a compact and lipstick in her purse and an overnight bag with her own clothes in the back. In the passenger seat next to her sat the girdle and nylons she could not imagine driving two hundred miles in.

It rained lightly all the way through the mountains of the Lincoln National Forest, but stopped by the time she reached White Sands. Laurie rolled down the window of her truck to let in the desert air sweetened by an early spring bloom of velvet mesquite and desert lavender. She noted a billboard that advertised the Agricultural College at New Mexico State University, one of the schools she'd applied to. She'd gotten her GED not long after Annie Kay was born, and she'd taken correspondence and community college courses to finish her first two years of college. Now she waited to see who would accept an almost thirty-year-old college junior. She didn't look forward to telling Annie Kay they'd have to leave Del Valle. But she'd deal with that once she found out if she'd been accepted anywhere.

It was almost 11:00 when she arrived in the little village just south of Las Cruces. She parked near the service entrance of the restaurant and went inside to use the restroom and put on her nylons. Back in the parking lot, she saw the light blue sedan Zibah had described parked next to her truck. Laurie tapped on the driver side window. A woman who looked about forty rolled it down, and Laurie greeted her with the code Zibah had given her, "I hope they have *obleas con cajeta* at the *panadería* today."

"They should be fresh." The woman gave the response Laurie expected, so she walked to the passenger side door and got in. "Thank you."

"When we get there, I'll drop you off and then go buy a few piñatas and some party favors so we have something to show for our trip across the border in case we get stopped on the way back. Have you been to Juárez?" the driver asked.

"Oh, sure, lots of times. I used to go with my grandmother and usually at least one of her friends when they went to the dentist. I guess old women with a car full of kids don't have to worry about attracting attention." She remembered how much fun she and Zibah had on their own at the market on Av. 16th de Septiembre. "My daughter and I go several times a year."

"Good," said the woman. "Because some women I drive haven't been, and I don't like listening to them talk about how dirty they think the city is. Or worry about getting mugged or attacked by a Mexican. Never mind that the doctors and nurses who are risking their reputations and freedom are Mexican. I'm going to listen to the radio," said the woman.

Laurie nodded and stared out the window. Zibah had told her there would be no need for polite conversation with the driver. The less they knew about each other the better. When the woman came to a stop at the border crossing, she rolled down her window and replied to the Border Patrol officer's question about her reason for entering Mexico, "A day of shopping, sir, planning my husband's surprise party."

Laurie hoped she looked calmer than she felt. He waved them through, and they drove to an area of the city Laurie was not familiar with. For several blocks it was residential until they reached a row of offices. Doctor Acosta. The name was on a list of doctors with practices in the building.

"When I get back, I will only go in to ask after you if I don't see you waiting on that bench." She pointed toward the plaza in the center of the offices. "Your appointment is for Anna Marina."

"Anna Marina," Laurie said the name aloud to the receptionist and heard how it could sound Italian as easily as Spanish and wondered if it was Zibah's creation for a woman who could pass. "*Tengo una cita.*"

"*No hay cita disponible,*" said the receptionist.

"Anna Marina." Laurie repeated the words again, hoping they would work this time. "I have cash." She slipped back into English and heard the desperation in her voice. She reached into her purse for the bills.

"Put that away," the receptionist said, her tone harsh. "I can't help you."

"Maybe one of the nurses . . ." Frantic, Laurie looked around the waiting room. "Can't someone contact him?"

The receptionist glanced around to make sure no one was in earshot. "Dr. Acosta had to leave. Quickly. Yesterday. No doctor here will see you. There are other . . ."

Laurie shook her head and stumbled out of the office, shoving the money back into her purse. She knew the receptionist was referring to one of the places downtown where she could get an abortion without an appointment. She'd heard of women who had gotten that kind. Some were damaged. Some were fine. Some died. She couldn't risk it. She was Annie Kay's only family. She composed herself and walked back outside to the small plaza. She followed the scent of little purple flowers growing near the fountain and sat next to a planter filled with dazzling orange dahlias beneath the shade of a large Montezuma cypress. She reminded herself not to attract attention and bit her lip to keep from crying.

When the woman arrived, Laurie hurried to the car. "The doctor was gone. The receptionist said he left in a hurry."

"Someone must have reported him. Get in." The woman prompted Laurie, who stood next to the door as though an alternative plan might emerge. "We have one other doctor here. But you'll need an appointment." She thought for a moment. "And he'll probably stop doing abortions for a while once he learns about Dr. Acosta. Get in," she said, "Now." She drove slowly away from doctor's office as Laurie put her face in her hands and wept. "We can look for someone else. There's Tijuana. But that's quite a trip." She stopped at a red light. When it turned green, she said, "Some doctors will do the procedure up to twenty weeks. You know who to talk to when you get home."

Laurie nodded and slouched against car door, pressing her face against the window like a homesick child.

"Border just ahead," said the driver. She'd driven slowly to give Laurie time to adjust to the facts. "Brush your hair, powder your nose. Put a smile on. Touch up that lipstick. We've done nothing illegal, but I'll drive again, and I don't want to give anyone cause to remember me or my car."

Laurie nodded and did as she was told. From the backseat a colorful burro piñata smiled at her in the mirror of her compact. They crossed the border without incident and returned to the restaurant. "I guess I'll just drive on home. No reason to stay overnight."

The driver nodded and drove away.

Laurie returned home along the same route she'd travelled earlier in the day. Uncomfortable, she tugged at the bodice of the starched dress. The buckle of its belt dug into her stomach, the garters pinched the flesh on her thighs. She needed to change. She pulled over in Tularosa—City of Roses the big Chamber of Commerce welcome sign read—and stopped at a diner, its peeling stucco walls decorated with images of bright red flowers. It was the place she'd always stopped with Estelle, who knew the geography of

Comanche Territory and told her the town was named for the red reeds that grew along the banks of Rio Tularosa, not for roses, the thorny bush planted by settlers.

Laurie grabbed her overnight bag from the back and went into the diner. At the counter she ordered a hamburger and a Coke then went into the Ladies Room where she put the small suitcase on top of the sink and kicked off the uncomfortable pumps. She unfastened the garters and rolled the false skin down her legs. Pulled off the stiff, confining girdle. She unbuckled the belt then unzipped the zipper that ran from beneath her left arm to her waist. She peeled out of the dress and stood in her bra and underwear, the respectable housewife in a heap at her feet. She sobbed, no longer caring about the attention she might attract. Then she wiped her eyes and pressed the buttons that released the levers on the suitcase. First she retrieved the beaded bracelet that had clashed with the colors of her borrowed dress and put it on before slipping into her soft jeans and pulling on a tight knit shirt Annie Kay had informed her was called a poor boy. They'd each ordered one from Sears catalog, Annie Kay's blue with black stripes, Laurie's maroon and beige. She picked up the woman she'd shed and shoved her into the overnight bag, went back to the counter, ate her burger, and drank her Coke.

As she neared Del Valle, she told herself she could get used to being married to Dan. She had to start thinking that way. When she told him she was pregnant, he would want to get married. That's the kind of man he was. Annie Kay's father was rich and white and could afford to pretend he didn't know that fifteen miles south of town, down by the Pecos River, deep in the country, Laurie Bow Kerchee raised her daughter with the help of the grandmother who had raised her. He graduated from the New Mexico Military Institute, went to college, and never returned. Dan Barlow was poor, white and religious, and of those three things it was the third that bothered her the most. He had ideas about a woman's place. He was judgmental and could be harsh. But he could also be fun. He worked hard. She couldn't love him the way she had loved Annie Kay's father. But she could not afford to raise another child on her own. And she would not turn her eleven-year-old daughter—the child who lived in the world with her, the child she'd do anything for—into a babysitter, a mother's helper. And it's what would happen. How could it not? She'd have to work even harder to provide for two children.

Just a few miles outside of town, Laurie read the billboard advertising the New Mexico Military Institute. Established 1891. Duty. Honor. Achievement. Men only.

When they were girls, she and Zibah had played going away to college the way some girls played dolls. They had to use their imaginations. Playing dolls meant feeding and diapering, dressing and undressing, spanking and teaching the baby how to be good. They did not know the routines of college life. Her grandmother, Estelle, graduated from Haskell Indian School, where she learned Poultry Science, but she refused to talk about Indian School, a place she had been sent. Zibah's grandmother Minnie chose to attend Bible College before she established her own country church. But Laurie and Zibah didn't ask about it. They heard enough about the Bible from Minnie as it was. From Zibah's cousin Wayman who went to the University of San Francisco on a basketball scholarship, they learned about college when he came home for holidays. But by then Annie Kay was three months old, and what she'd learned from Wayman didn't matter. Not yet, she'd told herself then, not yet.

But someday.

As she drove down out of the mountains into the farmland of the Pecos Valley, Laurie put her foot on the clutch and shifted gears. Her college fund would become Annie Kay's.

She remembered Zibah's words: *you can pass,*

She would pass for a woman who wanted another child, for a woman happily married to a man she didn't love.

She knew women who did.

Plenty did.

She could, too.

DOWNBURST

by
SOON JONES

In the morning darkness on my sister Ava Kim's birthday, I drive seven hours across state lines to my childhood home nestled in the countryside of Kentucky. When I pull up the gravel driveway shortly after noon, I'm the only one there.

Across the narrow, two-lane rural road are hundreds of sunken holes where there was once a forest, a few white clouds hanging mournfully over its grave. A man named Henderson bought up all the land around here after I left for college, dreams of a country suburbia dancing in his head. Soon houses will spring up like weeds.

My parents have already sold the field and moved back to the city about thirty miles away, and my half-brother Caleb got what was left. I should have fought harder for the farm, but I didn't.

Dust motes eddy around me in the old barn. I pick through my father's water-stained tools and take a shovel with good heft and a sharp blade.

Two trees which have grown so close together their branches twist and mesh separate our backyard from the field. The two-by-four swing my parents hung between them is still here, but the wood's rotted through, and it likely won't survive another storm.

I take a few steps past the trees and try to recall something I dreamed when I was a child. I wander deeper until the green ocean swallows me up.

I start digging where it feels right. The soil is dark and rich as cake, full of worms and centipedes and other slithering creatures. The shovel pierces through earth as easy as a knife through yielding flesh.

• • •

I turned seven on a Wednesday. When the presents had been opened, the cake eaten, and the other farmers had taken their children home, I sat by myself on the swing, looking out over my ocean, holding the new pocketknife Papa gave me in my hands. I caressed the pearlescent handle, traced the edge of the blade, both repulsed and excited by the possibility of being cut.

Caleb came up behind me and grabbed me by my shoulders, then yanked me backwards off the swing. My head hit the ground and the taste of iron exploded in my mouth and nose.

He took the knife away from me and said, "Knives are for boys. Here, I'll trade you."

He threw a spatula at my face, and the humiliation hurt worse. Then he laughed and walked away.

After dinner, we crowded in the living room to watch a movie. Ma was in the kitchen making more popcorn when Papa brought out one last present.

"Elise, why don't you come over here with that fancy new knife of yours and help me open this," he said, grinning wide.

Caleb glared at me from behind our father's head, and my tongue was thick and dry, swelling behind my teeth. This was the choice I hated most growing up: whose bruises would I rather bear?

"I lost it," I said.

Papa's smile faltered.

"What do you mean, you lost it?"

"I was out playing in the field and I dropped it. I can't find it."

Papa jumped up from the couch and grabbed my arm, yanking me up off the floor.

"You what?" he yelled.

Ma came running, yelling, "Franklin! Let go of her!"

Papa spun me around and spanked me with his bare hand, not even waiting to take me to my room first. Ava jumped up from the loveseat and clubbed him in the ear with her fist.

"Get your fucking hands off my sister!"

He slapped her across the face so hard her silver locket spun around her neck. Ma grabbed his arm and drew him back, and Caleb burst out laughing as they screamed at each other.

Papa had never hit Ava before. Because she was my mother's daughter, and not his, he was not allowed to punish her just as my mother was not allowed to punish his son. Either parent could hurt me, though, because I belonged to both of them.

Ava glared at Caleb, her face red and contorted, her nostrils flaring. She had never been afraid of him like me, and she had always been smarter. Quick as a rattlesnake, she pulled my knife out of his back pocket and threw it at my father's chest. Caleb stopped laughing as Papa bent down to pick it up off the carpet.

Ava banged through the back door. I chased after her into the fields.

"Ava! Come back!"

"Go back to the house, Elise," she yelled over her shoulder.

"You can't leave me with him!" I pleaded.

Ava came to me then and ruffled my hair.

"I just need a walk to cool down, okay? I'll be back soon," she said, and then left me adrift.

When I went back, Caleb's screams were echoing in our yard and Ma was smoking a cigarette on the back porch. It was the first and last time I ever saw her smoke. I sat beside her, and we watched

Ava disappear into the far reaches of the field, dipping beneath the horizon.

"I'm sorry about your birthday," Ma said, and then she laughed bitterly. "I left the city to get away from violence, not have it localized to my living room. If I'd known this was the way they did things in the country, I never would've left."

She smoothed my hair down on my scalp. Caleb stopped screaming. Somewhere in the house, Papa slammed a door. I fell asleep on Ma's shoulder, where I could smell her strawberry shampoo.

I woke up in my own bed with Papa sitting on the edge. He put the last present beside me, placing my knife on top.

"That's okay," I said. "I don't want it anymore."

Papa nodded and took them back into his hands. He stopped in the doorway, silhouetted by the yellow hall light, and said, "I love you, sweet pea."

I had a nightmare that night. There were monsters in the field, swaying and grunting together, and the sound of iron striking soft earth. I knew in the dream-sense way of knowing that if I went too close to my window, one of the monsters would drag me through the glass and do terrible things to me.

And then I was in a park chatting with a woman selling ice cream. She floated in the air with black and red balloons tied around her waist, and she looked like my sister, but older and sadder, and then she floated away from me.

In the morning after, Papa was on the phone saying things

like, "I know how teenagers are" and "I won't be angry, I just want to know," and my mother was crying on the couch.

I sat down at the kitchen table and Caleb took out two bowls, pouring us both cereal and milk. His right eye was puffy and there was a cut on his neck, peeking above the ribbed collar of his shirt.

"Where's Ava?" I asked.

He shook his head slowly and sat down across from me.

"Ava never came back last night."

Papa hung up the phone and went into the living room. Caleb and I didn't even touch our spoons as we eavesdropped.

"What did the Collins say?" Ma asked.

"Their boy Tom said Ava went to see him last night. She told him they should run away together, but he didn't think she was serious. Tom claims she went home after a while," Papa said.

"And the police?"

"They said they'd send a trooper out here tomorrow if she doesn't return by then."

Ma started crying again, and Papa shh-shh'd her.

"Don't touch me! You did this! You and your fucking son!" she snapped.

Caleb clenched his jaw and glared into his bowl. I stared at his nails.

"I'm going to make this right. I'm going to get in the truck, and I'm going to go looking for her. The Collins are already on their way. I'm going to make this right," he said again.

Papa left, and Ma stayed by the phone all day, jumping every time it rang. I went into the field and imagined finding Ava. She would be lying on the ground, and she would smile and tell me she was proud of me for being the only one smart enough to search the field. Then I would disappear into that green ocean with her.

Caleb walked out into the field after me, and even though I could hear him coming, I still jumped when he touched my shoulder.

"What are you doing out here, 'Lise?" he asked.

"I'm looking for Ava."

"You're in shock," he said, turning me back towards the house. "You go back inside with your Ma, all right? I'm going to take the four-wheeler and help Papa look for your sister. It'll be all right."

I let him walk me back to the house. I kept staring at his hands, at the dirt beneath his nails, the specks of dark brown smashed into his cuticles.

• • •

Clouds cover the sky like a thick film, and the wind is picking up. I'm sweating now, so I roll up my jeans and toss away my plaid shirt. My hair is plastered to my face with sweat. The muscles in my arms are burning, and my palms are raw.

The hole is up to my hips, then my chest. It's wide enough now you could hide a tractor inside. All I can see is dirt and the waves of grass above me, vibrant green against the dark gray of the sky. My body aches; I'm hungry and I'm thirsty. I should fill this hole and drive to a hotel before Caleb gets off work. I should forget about childish dreams.

The shovel strikes bone.

I drop on all fours and paw at the earth like an animal until I have a femur, cracked by my shovel, a tibia, some metatarsals, a spinal cord. A skull with a hole in the left parietal bone, fractures running down like rivers.

A necklace is tangled in the rib cage. My nails bend back when I try to open the locket. It's rusted shut, but patches of silver still shine, and on the back is a stylized *AK.*

I wrap the necklace around my fist, and my fist around the shovel. With my other hand, I twine my fingers around grass and roots and pull myself out of the hole, digging my toes and the blade of the shovel into the dirt to lift me up as the first drops of rain fall.

When I stand to my full height I see his truck first, parked half in the yard, half in the field, the driver's door wide open, the engine left idling. Then I see Caleb running towards me, parting the grass behind him, framed by the two trees in the distance. He's calling my name. He's making promises to explain himself. He's begging me not to tell our father.

The sight of him makes my lips curl. He still has that stupid fucking wispy blond mustache that he's been trying to grow out since last Thanksgiving. He once towered above me, but now he seems so small.

My blood boils and froths like waves smashing against the rocks. I grip the shovel tight with both hands and the wood bites into my palms. I shake with the promise of violence and whip the blade up over my head as my brother comes to me. Caleb's eyes are as wide as a fatted calf's standing before the butcher. I imagine Ava in the roiling storm clouds above us, and I wait for her signal. A torrent of rain suddenly crashes onto the remains of our farm.

And then, the thunder.

HEALTHY HEART

by
KASIMMA

The doctor said your grandfather was responding well to treatment before he "suddenly" slipped into the sleep of death. You decided against detangling the slip-into-sleep loom yet. What annoyed you was the word "suddenly." You scooped all the attention in your mind and emptied it on this Uncle in green scrubs. On a good day, you would have admired his coconut-brown eyes and his complexion that was as light as your wife's, but it was not a good day, so you focused on his head that was shaped like opioro mango.

"Well, wake him up," you said.

The doctor shook his head. "I fear he might never wake up. We are doing all we can, but his organs are shutting down."

You pulled your glasses to the tip of your nose and peered at the doctor as though you wanted him to see your own brown eyes.

He quickly added. "His heart is still beating. We cannot pronounce him dead until his heart stops beating."

"So there's a chance of survival?"

"It is extremely rare," he replied. "He is practically brain dead, which alone can count for death."

You sighed. "How long would it take for his heart to stop beating?"

He scratched his brows. "I don't know. I'm sorry. Your grandfather has such a healthy heart. Had he not had cancer, he might have lived over a hundred." He pulled his eyes away from yours, dropped them on his nails, and said, "I wonder if he made plans to or if he is an organ donor?"

"Excuse me?"

He flinched. His eyes darted like a pick-pocket's. "I apologise. I didn't mean to say that out loud."

Liar! He could not even look at you, could not even look at anything. He wanted the heart. He would not get the heart.

The desolation in you hunched your shoulders. Papa was suffering. You stiffened whenever his veins pushed against his skin as though trying to burst out. At ninety-two, he was strong, because you cannot even imagine enduring this level of pain at your forty-two. Cancer had turned his body into a pot of boiling tumors. If medicine had stage XX of cancer, Papa's would fall in line. It was as if they sent specialists according to their nationality to study Papa's case: American, Indian, Nigerian. Each one gave directions to the nurses, asking them to take blood samples and send tests on a race.

The thick smell of antiseptics in Papa's ward nauseated you. Tubes, lines, ports, catheters, oxygen masks, all attached to Papa, filling or draining his body. Papa was a piece of meat with a heartbeat. His skin became darker, scaly. But that godforsaken heart rate monitor kept zigzagging tales of his living heart. You fought tears.

"Sir, sir . . ."

Two nurses. Papa's offsetting smell must have clouded their perfumes, if they wore any.

"I'd like to administer your grandfather's drugs."

You leaned on the footboard rail. The nurses went about their businesses injecting poison, you hoped, into Papa's IV bag and arm. At least that would save him this pain. One of them gently raised Papa's head so that the other person would arrange his pillow. Papa's face remained corpse-like, but the veins on his arms and neck bulged, and he groaned. Your courage flew out the window. You tightened your fists on the rail to keep you from tumbling to the ground. You shut your eyes. Your tears tasted like Alomo Bitters. What kind of pain went home with death?

A soft, strong-willed hand helped you to the chair. You pressed your palm to your eyes until they almost popped. You released hold of your eyelids and waited for the blur to clear. The beep from the machines filled the room. One nurse, the fair-skinned freckled one, sat opposite you. If she dragged the spare wooden chair to you, you did not hear.

"Need water?"

You shook your head, gaining control. But that groan playing on repeat in your ear forced a fresh flood of tears down your face. You expected to hear her voice again, but you waited in vain. You checked to be sure she was still there. Her name tag read "Obot." She held out a tissue. You grabbed it and dabbed your eyes.

"I'm sorry," she said.

It was not her fault, you wanted to say, but it was. She was part of the problem. She was part of the people keeping Papa alive.

"He's in so much pain," you said.

"I know," she said.

You sniffed and looked into her eyes. "Help him. Nobody will know."

She squinted, dread blackening her face. "I don't understand."

Liar! "Give him more painkillers. He's in so much pain."

Her face relaxed. "He is already on the highest dose of morphine he can take. Any extra drop and I will be arrested. I will go to jail for murder."

It irked you that she sounded like the doctors. "Murder? A dead man cannot be killed, nurse. I thought he is already dead, nurse?"

If she was offended by your rudeness, she did not show it. "His heart is still very healthy. And until he is pronounced dead, he is not dead. But his case is new, and we are working on getting a solution to this."

"So he's your guinea pig?"

She closed her eyes, sucked in air, and breathed out hot steam that fried some of the hair on your arms. "We are trying to see if we can revive him."

"His organs are dead. His brain is dead. Even his flesh is dead. The only thing not dead in him is his heart. What, exactly, are you reviving, nurse? Cancer?"

She sighed again. You imagined her clutching on the gates of patience. But you wouldn't let it go.

"Give him a little more painkiller. He is in deep pain. Please." You joined your palms.

"I know this is hard for you." She touched your knee. "Try rubbing his feet, holding his hand, reading to him. Sing his favourite songs to him, reminisce about old times."

"So that what will happen?" you snapped.

She smiled, sighed, stood, left.

You allowed your thoughts to revolve around how to relieve your grandfather of his suffering. Your phone rang, shaking you out of your brooding. You dug the phone out of your pocket. Ngozi. You wanted to say the usual, "Hello, Ngozi," but your voice was buried deep into your stomach, and your skin was quilted with shame from your thoughts, and your eyes started raining.

"Hey, it's okay," she said.

Her voice was so soothing, always so soothing, that it made you cry harder.

"Don't worry. Don't worry, okay? I'm praying for you, for him, soon he will be put out of that pain."

She said other things you would later remember. You mentally subtracted six from the time on the wall clock to get Ngozi's time. She was supposed to be in class. Why was she calling? Did something happen?

"Ngozi, is everything okay? Is everyone okay?"

"Of course, why?" The "course" was dragged to oblivion.

"You're supposed to be in class."

"Dilibe." She paused. "Today is Saturday, Dilibe."

You slapped your forehead. What!

"I am very worried about you. Dilibe, should I come?"

"No, no. I am fine. You have classes."

"My students will be happy to take a break. My colleagues will not mind."

"The children . . ."

"Child, Dilibe. Child. A teenager even, not a child."

She sighed. "Dilibe, *ọ gini*?"

That was her voice of imposed calmness.

"Ngozi, I will be fine," you said.

"How is Papa?"

You sighed. "He's just lying there neither living nor dead."

"Shhh, he can hear you."

"Let him hear me. Not long ago . . ." and you downloaded the gist of the groan from death. Maybe your senses went on vacation, but Ngozi went to that city and brought them back. Then she asked to say hi to Papa. You put the phone on speaker and took it close to Papa's ear. She did not ask him the flat question of how are you. She did not go all bland, telling him to get well soon.

"Papa, if there is something we can do to help, please let us know," she said. "We love you very much, and we still want some more time with you. But we don't want you to keep suffering. Papa, it's okay to go."

The tower of Ngozi's strength and sensibility amused you. It made you realise your error, as you drove home, that your focus was on ending Papa's suffering instead of creating final memories. His children would not come, none of his grandchildren would come, but you were there, because you love him. Papa had been there for you since your birth. Everything you knew about your father, Papa told you. Papa fondly referred to your father as his child from his old loins. Papa told you how your father would have become a renowned surgeon if he did not get Maazi Okenyi's seventeen-year-old *anumpam* pregnant. Just for him to be in his house one day when they brought home the bloodied corpse of his son. Papa's voice would trail off, and he would shudder. He knew Okenyi's sons must have beaten his son to death. But he considered himself a weak man then, so he did nothing. But it dawned on him that if he continued to do nothing, his corpse would be the next to fall. And when the girl had you, they came and dropped you for him and sent her off to God-knows-where. He hoped hell. Papa pampered the existence out of you and it made your uncles and aunties and cousins jealous. Rumour said that Papa was responsible for the mysterious deaths of Okenyi and his sons. That Papa was deep-necked in black magic. That Papa did not go to church. True. That Papa was involved in money rituals. You saw a hardworking Papa whose wood business did well; a Papa who invested his profits in other businesses; a Papa who was generous to those who slandered him with his hard-earned money, which they dubbed "blood money."

• • •

When you received a call from your uncle that Papa was diagnosed with stage IV pancreatic cancer and had asked for you, you got on the next available flight from the United States. You met Papa asleep. And your uncles said, oh, no need to sit beside someone who's sleeping. The nurses are tipped to watch him. If he wakes or dies, they will inform us. And when you asked them if they didn't think it was a good idea to hold Papa's hand when Papa took his last breath? They laughed and called you an *Americanah*.

• • •

The tower of Ngozi's strength and sensibility amused you. When you got home, you did not turn on the light. No need. Nonsense. What was your business with hunger? You must have cried it out at the hospital. The smell of Papa's ward clung to your clothes, your skin. You undressed, threw your clothes into the washing machine, emptied your laundry detergent inside, like really, who cares if it's too much? Your penis slapped your thighs all the way to the bathroom. In the shower, you scrubbed your body one million times until your palms were sore. You sat crouched under the shower, your forehead on your knees. Papa. Your Papa. Young, you prayed with Papa most mornings using nzu and kola nut. Mama often flogged you for doing that and promised to cut off your ears if you told Papa. Once, at dinnertime, Mama refused to give you meat because you asked Papa this and that about Igbo spirituality which, according to Mama, was idolatry. Well, good for you, because Papa gave you all four pieces of meat on his plate. Papa sprayed you cash whenever you danced to Theresa Onuorah. To impress him, and win more money, you'd dress up colourfully like Onuorah's *Egedege* dancers. Mama admonished Papa for playing what she called devilish music. But Papa listened to Theresa Onuorah as though his life depended on her words.

Didn't Nurse Obot say something about songs?

You dashed out of the shower, flicked the switch, found your phone. Theresa Onuorah. It'd been so damn long! On YouTube, you typed "Theresa Onuorah" on the search bar, clicked on *Theresa*

Ojemba Enwilo, and spent the next eight minutes, pooling water at your feet, basking in nostalgia. Ah! Papa used to nod like a lizard to Theresa Onuorah's music. Hers was the only song he ever danced to.

• • •

You drove to the hospital the next morning, full of hope. You almost expected to see Papa awake and smiling. Rubbing his feet, you told him you brought him a surprise. Then you played Theresa Onuorah's *Egedege.* You dropped your phone in the empty mug on the table to amplify its sound. You sat on his bed and held his hand. You were looking at him, but your sight was in the past, on how Papa . . .

The bed shook.

You jumped.

Papa's left hand dashed to his neck with the speed of Hollywood ghosts. He scratched viciously.

Screams burst from your mouth. You ran out, shrieking!

"Calm down, sir," someone said.

Two nurses ran toward Papa's room. Heads poked out from the other wards.

"I'm fine," you said, shrugging off your rescuers.

When you returned to the ward, you met Papa, as usual, a slab of breathing meat. The nurses' faces asked questions: you answered.

"Oh, that's called reflex," one of them said, diving into a lengthy jargon. Their explanation did not cover why reflex did not happen since, why it happened after that you played *Egedege*.

Papa was trying to tell you something. You were sure.

The rest of the day found you taking backward steps in time. Something was keeping Papa alive. You did not want to concern yourself with why yet. *Egedege* filled your car on your drive home. You played it until you slept, played it while having breakfast, and kept playing it in Papa's ward. Something in that song prompted Papa's "reflex." If you were not so scared, you might have taken note of the particular second in the song when Papa jerked up, maybe that was where Papa's message was.

By the third day, your brain was fried in *Egedege*, so you called Ngozi. You had been afraid to tell her, because you thought she would find it ridiculous.

But she solved it. "It is a 'who,' not a 'what'?"

You froze. Where was your brain?

"Did Theresa Onuorah mention anyone in the song who might still be alive?" Ngozi asked.

"SHE is alive! Why didn't I think of this? You see why you are my better half?"

"What has she got to do with anything?"

"Everything! Maybe she knew Papa!"

Ngozi laughed. But it was not a laughing matter for you. You would not tell her that you plan to visit Theresa Onuorah. Ngozi was a staunch Christian, and you did not want her thinking that you were going to visit a water goddess as Theresa Onuoha was rumoured to be. Nothing in Theresa Onuorah's lyrics, at least all the ones you drowned your brain in lately, suggested anything "evil."

You kissed Papa's head. "Papa, I will be back. Let me go home and find a solution. I hope you guide me, Papa." You told him that *i hụrụ ya n'anya*, not the diluted English version of "I love you." You asked Obot could she please hold Papa's hand as often as possible? She looked unsure.

"Please." You held her hand. "I need to make a quick trip. I promise I am not like the others. I will be back. Just do this for me, please. I need him to feel a human touch, to feel he is not alone, just in case . . ."

She closed her eyes. When she opened them, they bore the assurance you needed.

• • •

It was already past one when you arrived in Unubi market square the next day. Unubi smelled of trees, water, dust. You'd had a rough day without food. You'd caught the first flight to Enugu at 9 a.m., then a three-hour bus trip to Ekwulobia. Tired of rickety buses, you mounted a motorcycle to Unubi. Next was to find Theresa Onuorah's house. You'd thought of the lie you'd tell when the time came. "You're a fan" sounded false, unless you're a ceiling fan because she hadn't released one song in decades. "You're a journalist" might sound scary. "You wanted her to sing at your grandfather's funeral." Perfect! Well, the person you asked for directions was nosy. You stuffed your story in along with some cash. He walked you to Onuorah's compound. You went in and knocked. A teenage girl in skinny jeans and a crop top opened the door. You smiled at her and introduced your true self and your fake story. She let you in.

The house was cool, maybe because it was spacious and scanty, or because your conscience pricked you for entering the house of a "heathen." The terrazzo floor gleamed, but it was not your business. You promised yourself never to remove your shoes. Well, the teenager did not mind. She showed you to one of the old, brown, suede cushions. You sat on another one just in case the one she pointed at was charmed.

She said let her see if the queen was willing to see anybody today. Shouldn't that have happened before you were even let in? She disappeared behind the flight of stairs. She did not seem afraid that you might steal? Why? Because they had supernatural powers or because there was nothing to be stolen? What would you steal? The stack of old VHS, the plasma TV, or the wooden staff with a lion's head? Anyway, whether the queen wanted to see you or not wasn't your business. You came with a sleeping bag.

It was almost noiseless, her footsteps, Queen Theresa Onuorah, the alpha and omega of Egedege, the only voice that made Alive Papa dance and made Sleeping Papa reflex. Your jaw dropped.

You lifted from the seat. She walked with the grace of a tiger. You expected her to be dressed in white gloves, a long shiny gown, beads on her hair, neck, hand, wrist, waist, and a long feathery hat, as she has worn in her music videos, but she was wearing a simple ankara gown. Her hair was covered with a slouchy, black, beanie hat. Her eyes lay down when she smiled. Her diastema, her small equal-height teeth . . . you were so in awe that you forgot your manners.

"*Nwa m, kedu?*"

You prostrated before her. She laughed, told you to rise, searched your eyes intensely. What was that in her eyes? Pity or a reflection of a mother's affection? She sat on the spot the teenage girl had pointed out to you, the spot you assumed was charmed, yes, that spot, that was where Theresa Onuorah sat. She pointed at your chair, and you perched on it. Old age had touched her, but you could not tell how deep.

"*A sị na nna gị nnukwu nwụrụ?*"

The pity you saw in her eyes then made sense. She thought you lost your grandfather.

"He's not completely dead yet, ma."

Her face scrunched up. You spilled your guts. She stayed silent, but you could tell from the two deep lines between her brows and the thinness of her eyes that she listened attentively. You reiterated that something in her song made Papa reflex, and you wondered if she could tell you what. She sighed, joined her fingers, lowered her head, closed her eyes.

After, maybe three years, she sat up, crossed her legs. "*Kedu ụka Papa gị nnukwu na-aga?*"

"Papa never set foot in any church," you replied.

She nodded. "*Enweghị m ike inyere gị aka.*"

Despair fell like a lump into your stomach. How could she say she had no strength to help you? Did you come to beg for strength or for help? She raised her palms. You took a cue and relaxed.

"*M ga-agwa gị onye ga-enyere gị aka.*"

You sighed. At least she offered to point you in the right direction. You were heading somewhere.

"*Ọ bụ dibia.*"

She looked at you, perhaps waiting for effect. You would later wonder if you were out of your senses when you accepted to go ahead, but at that point, you did not care if your helper was dibia, pastor, priest, imam, or the devil.

Theresa Onuorah only told you the dibia's name and that he was from Nnobi. Whether he was alive or dead, she did not know.

• • •

From Unubi, you went to Nnobi. Apparently, the family's surname was address enough. When you asked someone there for the dibia, they told you Prof did not come back this week and that you should go to his residence in Enugu and look for him.

The forwarding address led you to a big, white house on

Independence Layout in Enugu. It seemed too grand for a dibia's house, but you knocked anyway.

The gateman led you into a lush sitting room bathed in whiteness. A wooden altar of the Sacred Heart of Jesus hung by one corner of the wall complete with portraits of the Holies, rosary, crucifix. Anger built up in you because, for goodness sake, which day did ndi dibia start worshipping Jesus? But you waited because you knew this "farce" would point you in another direction.

A pleasant woman served you drinks. You thanked her, but drink was not your problem. Why were people so insincere? Why would someone make you journey back to Enugu when your solution could be in Nnobi? Theresa Onuorah would not lie. It's that man you met in Nnobi, that Uncle who gave you this Enugu address, that's the liar who must rot in hell.

Someone cleared their throat. You jumped to your feet. What was it with these people and noiseless walks? The man indeed looked like a professor. He must have been taller when he was younger. His hair and beard were as white as his home. He did not say a word until you said your greetings. Then he smiled closed-lip and stretched out his hand for a shake. His grip was strong; it reminded you of how fatigued you were.

"Sit down," he said. "So you've met Theresa Onuorah."

A cold chill blanketed you. Were you holding your drink at that time, it would have slipped from your hand. You did not remember mentioning Theresa Onuorah to anyone. Or had you?

"*Dilibe*?" Prof called you.

There was no drink in your mouth, but you had a gag reflex. You slapped your chest as you coughed.

"You should take some of that drink. It will help with the cough," he spoke calmly.

You did as you were told. Prof looked like he was stifling his laughter. You did not know what to answer. What was even the question?

"Tell me about your grandfather."

You looked at the altar of Jesus and at this man in a white kaftan. It did not make sense that he was a native diviner, but nothing in the past two months made sense to you. So, you told him everything. You answered all the questions Theresa Onuorah asked you to avoid wasting Prof's time and yours.

"Finish your drink first," was the only thing Prof said after your story.

"I am done, sir."

He stood. "Follow me."

You stood. He looked at your feet and looked at your face. You quickly pulled your shoes. He led you into a room lighted with a dim yellow bulb and smelling of blood. He asked you to sit and wait. There was no chair. You sat on the floor, as far away from the scary, bloody, wooden statues as you could get. Should you be here? Maybe you should have discussed this with Ngozi. But what in Heaven's name had Papa gotten himself into? Prof emerged looking more like a native diviner. He wore a piece of white cloth crossed from under his right armpit and thrown across his left shoulder. His left eye was smeared with nzu. He sat in a yogi lotus pose before you and commenced the *itụ nzu* ritual, connecting to the earth goddess and Her purity. Then he asked you,

"*Kedu ọjị ị jiri bia?*"

It hadn't occurred to you to come with kola nut. You opened your palm and shook your head. He sighed. He dipped his hand into a wide, small, clay pot, brought out one kola nut, and dropped before you.

"*Nke a bụ naira iri.*"

Was this man asking you to pay ten naira for the kola nut? Common ten naira? Okay, no problem. You gave him one thousand naira.

"*M sị na ọ bụ naira iri. Naira iri di n'akpa gị.*"

So he could even see the notes IN your pocket? You emptied your pocket, and there it was: a ten naira note. You straightened it and gave it to him. He dropped the money into another clay pot covered in red linen. He pointed at the kola nut on the ground and opened his palm. You picked it and returned it to him. He thanked you, turned to the statues, and said they should see the kola nut you brought for them. He sang a litany of names.

"*Kedu ihe ị kwo were bia?*"

But he was the same person you told your quest in the sitting room. Now he was speaking Igbo as if he could not speak English, asking you why you came as if he didn't know.

"I came because . . ."

"*Sụọ Igbo.*"

You switched to Igbo, reiterating that you wanted help to ease your grandfather's passing to the other side.

He frowned at you and shook his head. *"A bụrọ m dibia nsi."*

But, for goodness sake, when did you accuse him of being a dibia of evil or poison? Or did he mean dibia of shit? You explained why your intentions were pure. He nodded. Singing, he cast four strings of sixteen ugili seeds. He smiled, switching to a song of gratitude. You too offered gratitude. He kept a clay pot before you and poured gunpowder in it. He said he was going to the spirit land to see if your grandfather was there, and that you were not allowed to utter the word "death." What's your conceirn with utterance? But you reprimanded yourself, mindful that he read your thoughts. He lit the pot, held your right palm, and shut his eyes. You sucked in your lips and shut your eyes. But fear played a game of golf in your head. What if that fire over which he circled your hand burned you? What if there were spirits around you? It took a strong resolve to keep your eyes shut.

He called out Papa's name and said *"o mebigo,"* meaning he has spoiled, meaning Papa was already drinking palm wine with his ancestors in the spirit world while his heart stayed here in this world, beating drums.

You opened your eyes when he left your hand. He shifted the pot. The fire slowly died. He cast the ugili seeds and repeated his thanks. He turned stern eyes at you.

"Dilibe, gee m ntị ọfụma, ọfụma."

You listened attentively, attentively.

• • •

The next morning, you travelled to Achina, armed with keys, the dibia's instructions, and hope. Thankfully, no neighbour saw you arrive. The long gates did a good job of keeping your presence a secret. Your family's massive compound was covered in overgrown ata, but that was not your business.

You went upstairs to Papa's room, the dibia's step-by-step instructions playing in your head:

1. Shift the king-sized oakwood bed.

Sweat drizzled from your head as you reduced the bed to four logs of wood.

2. Peel the ash carpet out of the way.

3. Stand by the window, at the north of the room, and count five steps: one tile per step.

4. Break the fifth tile. You will see a wooden floor underneath.

So far, the dibia's instructions played out dead on. You dug out your hammer from your bag and shattered the tile. There was indeed a wooden floor with a rusty padlock marrying a hasp and lock. You knew then that you'd find what Dibia said you'd find. Fear coated you, sent your heart racing, but you shrugged it off. After all, Papa would do the same for you. You called Obot and pleaded with her to check on Papa.

She hissed. "Sir, I just came out from there."

"I am worried. Papa has always been there for me. I feel guilty not being there, and I don't know why I cannot shake this dreadful feeling away. I was wondering if you might be inclined to set a video recorder in his room? I just want to give myself the satisfaction that I never left him. I will be back tomorrow. I promise."

She sighed. "I will set my second phone on my tripod to keep videoing him. I have other patients to attend to."

You wanted to remind her that you wished she would hold his hand too, but in the absence of puff-puff, puff will do. After ringing off, you landed one angry blow on the padlock. It gave way. You raised the door. Dust and darkness greeted you.

5. You will need to go with a torchlight so you don't trip on the stairs.

You flashed the light on the staircase, leading to an underground. You made the sign of the cross and headed downstairs. It smelt stale and moist.

6.   On the east of the room is a black curtain. Pull it.

Once your feet descended the last of the ladder, you flashed the light to the east of the room. A black curtain stood menacingly. Your heartbeat took it upon itself to deafen you. You imagined a strange creature standing there, holding a bloodied axe, mouth dripping blood, screaming, "I need blood! BLOOD!" as you've seen in Nollywood movies.

You shook your head, but the bloody thoughts clung to you. Your body trembled. If someone would need any bloody blood from any bloody place, Dibia would have bloody prepped you. Emboldened, you darted to the curtain:

dragged it aside:

stepped back:

flashed your light.

It was just as Dibia said: a beating heart, no, not the smiley-shaped heart, a heart-shaped heart.

7.   *Igwọ ike ji ndụ* is what your grandfather did. You will see the ọgwụ swinging back and forth, imitating a beating heart. Provided that *ọgwụ* is hanging, the owner's heart will continue beating even if their flesh rots and melts away and they turn into a skeleton. But once the *ọgwụ* touches the ground, its owner dies at once.

No wonder the pains Papa went through to hide it. No wonder the pain he now suffers. You called Obot again. Before you could say a word . . .

"Sir, I am currently in his room to give him his injection. The video has been recording."

"Thank you," you said.

You needed that video to compare the time of death of the real heart and the charm-heart. Covering yourself in the blood of Jesus, you took scared steps, unhooked the heart from the nail, and dropped it. It slowly beat to a stop. What did your eyes just see? Was this a dream or what did your eyes just see? Your pocket vibrated, startling you.

"Nurse Obot?"

"He's gone," she said, barely audible.

She was saying something, maybe sorry or what, but you imagined yourself going back to Unubi to offer gifts to Queen Theresa Onuorah then to Enugu to thank Prof then back to the United States. Papa was finally peacefully asleep. He would no longer suffer. You slid to the floor.

If your sobs were a drum, it would be udu.

CAMARO

by
ARAH KO

You've seen so many people, you could never count them all, but this is the one you remember. Her mascara was smudged in the same way your mom's did after she talked to your father; her eyes were bruises. She might have looked young if she wasn't so miserable. She was brushing her teeth at the RV drinking fountain right between the bathrooms and your mother's 1981 Chevy Camaro. Her mouth was bright red, with lipstick, maybe, or blood. As her hand moved, the color smeared across her teeth, the brush, her index finger. You and your brother stared, but she didn't notice you watching.

"Boys, you ready to go?" your mom called. It was less of a question and more of a statement. Jason popped the passenger's seat over so you could climb in the back. Mom shoved the key in the ignition, knocked back the last of gas station coffee, and twisted the key. The engine of the car that used to be your dad's sputtered to life, swerved on the gravel, roared onto the road.

It'd been a few thousand miles since you lost your name. It used to be the same as your father's, but it became harder and harder for your mom to say. There were days she tried to sound it out, stuttered over it, then she gave up entirely.

"Son," she said, firmly, somewhere outside of Tucson. You had been parked at pit stop, squinting at a thorny forest of saguaro but turned to blink at her, at your new name. "You've got a hole in your pants," she said. "C'mere." You came. She whipped a tiny sewing kit out of the glove box, threaded the needle with bright red string and sewed them up right there. You watched the wind wave through the furry-looking cacti, the bruised, bluish mountains. Jason laughed at your face the whole time.

Four thousand miles before that was the last time you spoke to your dad. It had been on a gritty payphone in Alberta, which your mom says is in Canada, but Jason thinks must be in British Columbus, wherever that is. You clenched the phone between white fingers, remembering the vendetta your mother had developed against quarters, the way her mouth pulled down at the corners whenever she drove by a phone booth.

Jason never wanted to talk about your father, let alone to him.

"Don't you remember what he did?" Jason snarled the last time you asked, shoving you in the shoulder. His eyebrows were dark and familiar, furrowed on his forehead. He searched your face for something he didn't find. "You're just a kid," he said, disgusted, and followed your mom into the gas station, leaving you behind.

"Moses," your father said when he answered. You did not know if he could tell it was you from your breathing, or your older brother's general reluctance to talk to him. "How are you?"

"I got to ride in the front seat today," you said, because you couldn't say "good." Your mom had washed your hair in a public restroom with baby soap that morning. Jason had eaten the last Slim Jim. British Columbus was cold.

"Wow, little man." Your father sounded like he disapproved but was proud at the same time. "You must be getting big." You breathed together for minute; you liked the sound of your father's breathing. "Moses," he said at last. "Tell me where you are, buddy."

You heard the phone give you a "time's up" warning. You watched the corner of the street, knowing your mom would come around it any second, remembering her desperate questions that first night on the road. *You want to be together, right?* She had said. You had been sleepy, squinting at the passing streetlights, your brother's nervous shifting. *Then we have to stay here, in the Camaro.*

You fingered the last coin sitting at the bottom of your right pocket. "We're nowhere, dad," you said, watching the sun set red on the horizon.

You learned how to sleep on the road many miles before that. It had only taken several states—a few hundred miles—to get used to living in the car. You kept a toothbrush in the seatback pocket. Your pillow had dinosaurs on it, and Jason's was speckled with astronauts. Mom owned four CDs and could only bear to listen to two of them, so you knew each word of the Beatles by heart. You collected toilet paper rolls at public restrooms when you could and ate fruit from trees at the side of the street. After a memorable patch, when your mother worked evenings at a diner in Georgia and you lived in less-ratty motel, you always ordered cheeseburgers with no pickles for dinner. You and Jason argued about everything: the color of the sky, the names of the birds, who made that scratch on the left door of the car. When you were on the road, your favorite thing to do was ride shotgun, even when your mom was in a mood, so you could count the miles the Camaro ate up accumulate on the odometer.

Despite this, you had lost count of how many miles you'd been through when your aunt gave in. Your mom would stop by her sister's house every few months, get a good shower, eat some whole grain toast, and ask for money. On one of those weekends, she was just coming out of the bathroom when you saw the lights flashing red and blue on the lawn.

"Mom!" you yelled. "What do we do? Where do we go?" Your mom went wild, leaping on her sister, nails tearing rabidly into her face. Your aunt shouted back, "You can't keep doing this, Sharon! You can't!"

Jason's face, you remember, had gone blank like an open road. He pulled you into a corner and hid your face in his shirt. You stayed there until the yelling stopped, until a tired-looking man in a white button down coaxed you to another car, another road, another life. You lived with your aunt, who moved into a small, sunny apartment with sixties-style furniture, far away from highways. When you started school again, Jason told the principal your aunt was your guardian because you were orphans, and you didn't correct him.

Now you live in Washington, some thirty minutes outside of Seattle. The weather is mostly the same; the landscape never changes. You keep the beat-up '81 Camaro under a tarp in your tiny garage because, despite years of therapy, you still have the urge to sleep in it.

Jason flies out every few months—you never visit him because he's always moving. Your aunt called him "tetherless" once, which sounds about right. On good days, when it doesn't hurt to remember, you think your mom was not tetherless, that maybe she had the opposite problem and saw that line chasing right behind her through the rearview mirror.

This time when Jason comes, he seems restless, itchy beneath his skin, so you rip the tarp off the car and drive him down to Saltwater State Park. You plant your brother on a chunk of driftwood next to a six-pack of beer, and you sit there for two hours, just drinking and listening to each other breathe.

"You remember that woman?" you ask suddenly. "The one at the RV stop with red lipstick on her teeth." It wasn't what you meant to say, but you find yourself waiting for the answer.

Jason raises one eyebrow at you. "You mean the one with the toothbrush?" he asks. You nod, surprised he remembers the same woman you remember, one of thousands. Maybe more. He turns to look back at the sea, squints from the sun.

"Huh," he says. "I always thought it was blood."

CHICKEN

HUSBANDRY

by
ARAH KO

You help prop up two plastic folding tables on the lawn and dress them in black twenty-gallon garbage bags. Aunt Em rolls up her sleeves and hoists a vat onto a propane burner, fills it with water from her garden hose. The burner *click click clicks* to life, and the low bubble fades into the background. The gas stings your eyes.

You asked for this. You decided at the age of nine when your mom left your dad in Chicago and moved back in with her parents in Hawaii, giving you a dozen chicks in his place, that if you couldn't do this you had no business eating meat, or raising animals, and should probably leave the island altogether. You weren't born here, in the jungles and pastures, but you know what it takes for a transplant to wither. And it was wasteful to shoot the extra cocks with bb pellets and leave them in the cane grass to rot. So when the time came to process this year's extra flock, you volunteered.

In the backyard, twenty-two chickens squat in a mesh pen on the bright green grass, their bodies slashes of auburn, white, gray. They've been fasted for two days; you resist the urge to feed them one last meal.

Aunt Em's then-husband kills the first one. In the years that follow, you'll forget his name. It's from him you learn the objective is to be quick about it. Once the neck is stretched on the wood-block, you slice quickly and with your sharpest knife. The quicker and sharper, the more merciful, the less violently the body jerks when you hang it upside down to bleed. The work is hotter and messier than you expected, their beady eyes—unbearable to look at. Chicken blood spatters on your clothes, dries to brown.

The next part is the worst. Aunt Em seizes the blooded rooster with one rubber-gloved fist and plunges the bird into the pot of boiling water. After that, the scent of singed hair will always make you gag.

Once loosened, the sopping animal is plopped in front of you on the folding table. You rip handfuls of nasty feathers from the bird—they pop out at the quill, ooze a yellow liquid. You recognize the last of the roosters by its lovely coloring, speckled, with feathered feet. You raised it from a chick, its feathers downy like a cotton ball, eyes dark and shiny. He was always at his brother's throats, biting and scratching you, one of too many roosters disrupting the careful balance of the flock. *A bad husband*, Aunt Em called him.

After that, it gets better. A defeathered chicken looks more like meat. It's easy enough for you to pull the organs out, save some for stock, careful of the yellow-green bile pouch. When Aunt Em applauds your unflinchingness, says you're nothing like your father, you flush with pleasure. At the praise, you pick up steam, say, "It's almost like cooking!" severing the knees at the tendon, scraping the lungs out with your fingernails. You cut open one rooster so perfectly, two white testicles roll out and bounce on the table. You laugh. It's funny.

Then it's done. Aunt Em bags the birds in clear plastic, and you toss them into a cooler. They'll go to feed four families this season, one of them yours. You hose fluid and loose feathers off the tables, satisfied that you belong here. Bloody water soaks into the ground.

Years from now, you'll be surprised at how much you miss this moment, how you'll come to hate the glossy, clean packages of processed meat in your urban Whole Foods. The way you pretended you could taste the earth, worms, and rotten sweet potatoes your chickens ate as you devoured their muscular, baked thighs. The messy dignity of looking your food in the face and knowing what it costs beyond the sticker label.In the backyard, Aunt Em lights a cigarette that will prove to kill her, sucks dark smoke into her lungs, blows it out through both nostrils. She tells you something then you choose not to remember, will regret not remembering. You're busy. You're thinking about your living flock, mostly egg-layers, all of them beautiful: Light Brahmas, Partridge Cochins, Silver-laced Wyandotte. What are they doing now? Nosing through the compost, probably digging up your mother's garden. One hen is broody, fluffed up on a nest. She trusts you so much, she lets you count the eggs with your fingers, one by one.

OARSMAN WANTED

by
JOE MILAN JR.

When night drizzle shimmered in the beacon lights, Dad manned the rudder while we rowed the one-eighth replica Viking ship East across the bay. We took it up a stream with tall-boy-littered banks and beached just behind the Ninety-Nine Cent Value Dream. Then we raided the dumpsters. Our plunder: expired cans of Spam, moldy boxes of band-aids, and battered bags of Gold Rush brown rice. Raids after holidays were best. Freezer-burned Thanksgiving turkeys and Independence Day charcoal we fed Dad's salvaged Franklin stove. In the old world, Dad had been something of a carpenter or an engineer—something to do with his hands—so when he found the half-built boat under a rotted tarp behind our duplex, dragon head at the prow and all, it manifested obsession.

On nights when Dad wasn't working a double, swabbing hospital floors, he was in the EZ Assemble shed water-sealing the boat. During World Cups, the uncles and mom chanted "대한민국!" at the TV, and Hojun, Sohee, and I muttered, "go Korea," but Dad stayed alone in the shed, bleaching and sewing scrap blue jeans for sails. For birthdays we got newly carved, larger oars with sneaker sole handgrips. Our raids went farther upstream, but all we found was much of the same—trash bags of expired cans. When Mom caught Hojun sneaking in the window well after curfew, Dad said, "Get your oar." Between the groans of the hull on the dark waters, he muttered in Korean *Destiny is in the bins*—or maybe it was—*His arms are bins.*

Going to college, I struggled to translate lies about why college was too far for me to make it back in time for the raids. On one of my trips back, Sohee's high school boyfriend cornered me to ask if Dad was serious about him rowing.

We grew up, got out, got married, and became doctors and lawyers. We learned to ignore our own children with night pillagings of paperwork we brought home to tunnel dark rooms. Dad tried recruiting from the Korean church, but those who weren't too old wouldn't be caught dead on a rowboat. One summer Dad sailed around the bay in the daylight for Seafair with guys from the

Norwegian association—even dressing up as a bullet-headed Viking with horns and all. But after that, the boat ran aground in the front yard with a big sign, "Oarsmen Wanted."

The sign faded. The hull collected spray-painted dicks from roaming high school kids. After Mom died, he hung her favorite teakettle from the dragon's mouth and her photo on a single shield on the port gunwale. A few months later, he painted the boat bright yellow and blasted the Beatles' "Yellow Submarine" from one salvaged boom box and some ancient Korean opera from another. More particleboard shields sprang up on the gunwales, each with painted portraits of flocks of birds and pods of dolphins and smiling stick figures with indiscernible titles of mixed Korean, English, and—I guess—runes. Then he hung from the cross beam of the mast a gold piggy bank on one end and on the other an olive branch.

He died at work while swabbing in a bathroom. They found him leaning against the wall, stiff as a plank and supported by his mop and the Airblade hand dryer. It was a "no" from the county to burn Dad and the boat out on the bay—we were relieved—and instead we left it at the dump and scattered his ashes behind the Value Dream.

———

TO KEEP
THE MIND
QUIET

by
JACOB MONIZ

In the summer that my mother killed herself, I'd been away for just a year. It was a sense of obligation that convinced me to return, the impetus being some repairs and general maintenance at her apartment complex that had been causing her stress. The landlord was a piece of shit. After barely making it through high school, I'd been offered a job doing some construction work for a friend's father up in Glenn County, up north in Willows. Over time, I got good at it. The work was tough and didn't leave me time for much else, but it tired my body and kept the mind quiet.

I worried when it got too loud.

The trip from Willows to Modesto was three hours long, but the route itself had only three directions to follow, hardly any turns. That meant a lot of time alone with myself and memories of home, memories for which I rarely made the time. In particular, I thought about the dogs that used to roam around the neighborhood. The place was filled with strays, dogs abandoned or set loose by selfish, careless owners too fucked-up for pets. When I was fourteen, I took a shaggy, pepper-haired stray back home with me. She was the most pathetic-looking of the lot. I fed her a package of lunch meat, turkey, I think, and drew her a bath, playing with her as the water did its work to wash away the fleas and dirt matted on her fur. She was looking pretty good, but when I went to towel her off, she shook, and then her eyes rolled backwards in her head. My mom came home and found me sopping wet and crying in the bathroom with this random dog panting frantically in my lap. She helped me wrap the dog in a towel, then called animal control to take it away. When they arrived, they wrinkled their foreheads in pity and told me that she probably had parvo.

Anyway, that was running through my mind on my drive to Modesto. Haven't bothered much with dogs since. I saw a few as I arrived at my mother's neighborhood. Like avoiding an ex at the supermarket, their presence forced me to take the long way round to my mother's apartment. I entered without knocking. We were family, and I knew I was expected.

"Mom?" I spoke into the empty apartment. Everything was yellow: the peeling laminate floor, the walls, the single-pane windows. Yellow is the sign of age, the quiet passage of time.

"Hm?" She answered from her bedroom. I didn't know her mood at present, so I approached carefully, stopping short outside her bedroom door.

"Did you take your meds today?"

"What a way to greet your mother." She paused and waited for me to respond. I stayed quiet. "No, hon.' I don't need it. I told you, that shit makes me heavy."

"Well," I said, only mildly concerned. She seemed calm, at least. "How about dinner? You hungry?"

"I don't know, Hunter. I'm waiting for my body to communicate that information with me."

I took a step forward and pushed open the door to the bedroom. My mother stared upward, eyes unmoving as she took in the curves and colors of the tapestry above her bed, yellow, orange, and red. Thick terry cloth fabric hung weighty against the nails hammered haphazardly into the edges of the tapestry, which had been purchased at a roadside in Arizona during one of my mother's unplanned excursions. She'd called me the day she got it, rambling on about its similarities to some imagined tapestry of her fictional past. I might have continued to interrogate her on her health, but the odor of skunk that permeated her space communicated to me that her lethargy would soon give way to hunger. Mom was a stoner, which was better for her than being sober, and actually one of our very few shared interests. I left for the kitchen and pulled out the phonebook, then dialed for take-out. Meds were more appealing when offered with a meal.

A collection of orange pill bottles covered my mother's countertops, both empty and full. Labels like Loxitane, Seroquel, and Clozaril were printed in emboldened black print, each expressed as more a statement than a name. My uncle used to say that the woman who laughed to herself was not the sister he grew up with, but I could never imagine her any other way. I only ever knew my mother as the woman who laughed to herself, cried to herself, saw every action taken by others as some injustice committed against herself. My mother was the aged musician who claimed music executives had stolen her work, the woman checked periodically into the hospital because she wouldn't stop screaming that Kirk Hammett was framed for the murder of Laci Peterson.

Metallica fans were rioting.

After calling in an order for Chinese, I stepped out into the thick heat of the Central Valley, dry and arid and made all the more worse by smoke drifting ominously from perpetual wildfires. My mother's decrepit apartment, paid almost entirely by government assistance, overlooked a patch of yellow grass and faced the local community college I'd refused to attend. Beyond that, thousands of acres of almond orchards stretched out across the valley, pink and full in spring, but nude and barren by summer.

"Those motherfucking almond trees make me rage," my mother used to say. "It just doesn't make sense to be growing almonds here. It takes so much water. It's fucking nuts!"

She'd made that joke when I told her my plans to move north, smoke drifting from a cigarette in her left hand as she lounged in a frayed and faded lawn chair, something between a chuckle and a cough emphasizing just how taxing humor could be.

"Hunter, why don't you just stay? You're gonna go all that way and do what, patch up some drywall? Stay here, Hunter. Go to school there, right here, Hunter. You can stay. You don't have to go."

She'd almost convinced me. For some inexplicable reason, even the slightest moments of coherence and sanity could trick me into believing that my mother was normal. It could be different, I thought. I can go to college. Sure, she'll need my help sometimes, but we're family. I can help her. This can work.

It didn't. That same night, lying on dampened sheets soaked through with the sweat of summer heat, I listened as my mother's manic rambling disassembled the fantasy. Her voice carried from her bedroom, dancing wildly throughout the apartment.

"Nosey Hunter, goddamnit goddamn, Hunter. I'll make you sorry, make you damned sorry, Hunter! I was the belle of the ball, yes I was! Oh, yes I was. Long before that bitch, that little bitch. Gonna fuck her up."

I knew what would come next and closed my eyes, lying on top of my sheets, muscles motionless and tense. After several hours of exhausted crying and laughter, my mother grew silent. A few minutes passed, and I heard the click of my door being opened. I could feel her standing in the doorway, a presence staring in the dark.

"She broke it. That little cunt broke it."

I said nothing as my mother walked toward my bed. She sat down next to me and placed her left hand on the inside of my thighs, fingers moving slick and slow against the sweat.

"Be more quiet than the most quiet you have ever been in your entire life."

I didn't move, and I didn't speak. I tried to ignore her. To fight would be to acknowledge.

I kept my eyes closed, but felt my mother's hot breath against my lips as she opened her mouth and kissed me. My lips pursed and I imagined I was somewhere else, fighting the cry that welled in my chest in hopes that my mother would think me asleep. My mind was loud.

Moments passed. A small cry escaped from deep within my mother, both devoid of and filled with meaning. A noise with meaning only I could understand. Her hand stopped rising between my thighs, stopped just beneath the point of no return. It seemed like she was waiting. For what, I'm not sure. Eventually realizing that I wouldn't respond, that I wouldn't wake to engage with her behavior and partake in the performance, she climbed from my bed and stood solemnly in the doorway.

"We're going to break tradition, Hunter. Break the cycle."

I left the next morning. After it happened, I think I had a dream, though it may have been a thought. I don't remember falling asleep. I just remember my uncle and the two of us on a hunting trip. We're aiming at a buck in September, and he's telling me to be more quiet than the most quiet I've ever been in my entire life.

The Chinese was delivered about a half hour after I called. I walked into the apartment and threw the bag of food down upon my mother's crowded card table, blind as my eyes adjusted to the dark.

As they did, my mother came into view, standing in her doorway down the hall, staring at me sadly.

"Dinner, mom. I ordered Chinese."

She nodded her head. "Good, hon'. I'm hungry as a hostage."

We ate. She took her meds. I did my duty as a son and made repairs to the apartment. At the end of the week, I left Modesto, making empty promises to visit as my mother begged me to stay. These promises were made at a distance, both literally and figuratively. I turned my back to leave. Before I'd made it past the door, my mother snuck a hand onto my shoulder and squeezed it tight. It was the first time she'd touched me since that night in my bedroom. I didn't turn back, and she didn't follow me out.

As I drove through the city for what I knew would be the last time for a long time, I realized I'd made a wrong turn. Lost in a maze of one-way streets and dead-end turns, I didn't notice the pack of dogs about to run in front of my car. I saw them at the last second and slammed on my breaks, cursing as they weaved in and out of traffic, but grew quiet at the sight of a shaggy, pepper-haired stray. She was smaller than the one I'd known, a pup. I sat, idling in my car, and watched as she ran with her friends until they'd gone completely out of sight. I found my route pretty quickly after that, but thought again about dogs as I made my way to Willows.

Three weeks later, I got the call that my mother had died. She was found by my uncle dead in the tub, a glass coated in antifreeze set carefully on the tiled floor I'd sealed just weeks before with grout.

I don't remember crying, though I'm sure I must have. My uncle offered to make arrangements for a funeral and would send me my mother's things, but I didn't like the idea of him invading her space. I remembered my dream, my uncle's hands gripped tight along the rifle, the stock against his shoulder, eyes trained squarely on a buck. I remembered him whispering to me. Over the phone, I lied and told him that I'd pack her things on my own. Later, I left a message for her landlord asking him to trash or donate her belongings.

I didn't return to Modesto for a while, but when I did, it was the springtime and almond blossom petals blew in the wind, catching the sunlight in shades of pinks and whites. I was on my way to a job in the country, in the orchards, and it was the first time I felt that I could breathe deeply in the valley. I took it all in and imagined that the trees never changed, that everything would stay that new. The thought was loud. It was like music, and I let it sing.

WHISKEY
TO THE
WOUND

by
RACHEL NUSSBAUM

I didn't know I was immortal until my arm was being hacked off my shoulder.

Honestly, it happened because I'm a drunk fucking mess. The car had already passed us once down the saddle road. It was the usual crowd, white trash wasted on a Friday night and walking from the pub to someone's cabin with the promise of more alcohol. Eventually, we realized it was midnight and another eight miles away, so the majority of the group turned back to town.

"Whatever, pussies," Janet said. It was her family's cabin. "I don't *get* tired."

"Bitch, we don't *sleep*," Arin slurred, totally plastered.

Me? I was drunk and moody, and I just wanted to punish myself like I usually do. So I stumbled through the night with two kids from my old graduating class. I didn't know them particularly well—but like me, they were permanent fixtures of the only pub in town, and tonight they were offering Wild Turkey.

That was more than enough for my dumb ass.

It happened when we'd stopped for Arin to piss. Janet squinted down the road and frowned.

"Didn't that car pass us earlier?"

They revved the engine and tore down the road, right into Janet. She folded in half like a paper doll, and her body flew off the shoulder into the woods. Before the bile even worked its way out between my lips, a pair of arms yanked me into the car.

Still drunk and dizzy with panic, I faded in and out. I was yanked from the vehicle. Dragged into a cabin. Thrown into a tub. Pain dug me out each time I thought I'd escaped into unconsciousness. I looked down at my naked torso; they were slicing into my side, they pulled this goey, pulsating lump out of me and oh fucking *fuck* it was my kidney.

I shouted. I flailed and kicked, trying to push them away.

"Put him out of his misery, fuck." One cursed.

His friend picked up an axe by the door.

Each swing sent a new wave of blinding agony through me. A

hit to my chest knocked the air from my lungs. Then my arm. They hacked away at my shoulder mercilessly, my tense muscles snapped apart like rubber bands. When the blade splintered and broke through bone, I screamed so loud I vomited again. More bile, and blood now too.

I wasn't passing out. Wasn't dying. All I could do was feel. Feel the alcohol-induced numbness I'd carefully cultivated over the years rip apart like tissue paper. Eventually, my arm slid down the tub and the jagged stump squirted blood in their faces—I was a sobbing, whimpering mess in a pool of my own fluids. And it would have been a fitting end for me—if it would just. Fucking. End.

"How is he fucking still alive?!"

Out of the fuzzy corners of my vision, I saw a log fly out from behind his head. It cracked as it made contact, and he dropped the axe.

And in the next instant, Arin was there, and he scooped up the axe and brandished it wildly.

"Who wants a piece?!" he yelled. "I will fuck your shit up!"

A face hovered over me.

Janet.

Her lip was split, and her front teeth were missing. My head bobbed, and I realized her body wasn't straight. She was twisted at the spine, legs facing to the side.

"You're okay now, Derek." she said, wincing as she bent down to pick up my arm.

• • •

We drove the sickos' stolen car to Janet's cabin. I found out later Arin had killed one of them with the axe. Once I had healed, I helped bury the body.

But I'm getting ahead of myself.

Janet laid me out on the floor before pouring some whiskey down my throat and taking a big chug herself. I watched in absolute horror as she braced herself against the wall and Arin gripped her torso and twisted her spine back into place.

"Fucking OW!" she yelled.

"Sorry," Arin mumbled. "You good?"

"Ugh. Yeah."

Janet cracked her neck and looked at me.

". . . I don't really know where to start with this," Arin said.

"Grab my sewing kit."

They waited for the alcohol to kick in. Janet gave me a towel to bite as she got to work stitching up my wounds. Arin hopped back and forth, asking me if I needed anything to drink, or if I wanted to watch TV while we waited.

"You're doing great, man," he said as Janet finished closing the gash on my side.

My arm was a bit harder. Janet unwound two rolls of duct tape trying to secure it. Pain radiated through my stump the whole time, but when we were done, I could feel the tingle of my limb return.

"...Too soon to ask for a fist bump?" Arin asked.

Janet smacked him.

They explained it as best they could while they helped me onto the fold-down futon. Janet found out when we were sophomores, during a hunting accident with her uncle. Arin found out about it in our senior year, when he crashed his jeep off a bridge.

"...How did you know...me too?" I mumbled when I finally found my voice.

"I think it's everyone from our graduating class. Going theory—everyone who went on the class trip to Alaska in freshman year," Janet explained.

The class trip. There were twenty-one of us who raised the money to make it.

"You know how Mr. Murphy said it was super crazy rare to see the northern lights in May?" Arin asked. "And how they were insanely swirly and bright?"

"I didn't make the connection until Arin's accident, but now I'm pretty fucking sure whatever that was, it wasn't the northern lights. And it changed us."

I looked down and blinked at my body. My fingers were twitching. My shoulders were shaking.

"Derek?" Arin asked. "What just happened was so, SO fucked up, but I...it's gonna be okay, you know?"

His hand hovered over my good shoulder. Janet passed me a bottle of water then, and she held it to my mouth as I drained it.

"Don't leave me alone tonight," I whispered.

"Course not," Janet promised.

• • •

Janet, Arin, and I had graduated three years ago. We didn't know each other well—sometimes ended up in the same booth at the diner, but so does everyone when your graduating class is forty kids. I always wondered why they hadn't gone on to better things. Those who get trapped to rot here, their parents either run a business in town or they grow weed out on the ridge. Guilted into staying, inherit a business you never wanted.

I'd wanted to get out—I just couldn't find a college that would take me. And that had hit me hard back then. I turned to alcohol very quickly. Numbing down the sadness that crept up every time I remembered I was still here.

For a long time, I thought I was cursed.

In a way, I was right.

It took a day for my arm to reattach itself. Janet said it would probably have grown back, like her missing teeth (and apparently my stolen kidney) did, but she didn't know how long it would take.

I drank more in those few days than I did since graduation. The haze was barely enough to numb the pain of healing, but I was so drunk I didn't care.

". . . You don't think they'll go to the cops, right?" Arin asked after we finished burying the body.

"Not a chance," Janet said, lighting up. "They'd out their operation."

"Who were they?" I asked. "This stuff happens in cities, but out in the boonies?"

Janet held up her joint.

"This is the Emerald Triangle. You know how many people get illegal jobs trimming?" she asked.

I nodded. I'd spent summers trimming myself.

"Did you know more people go missing up here than anywhere else in the state?"

Fuck. I'd seen missing people posters, but I didn't think it was that bad.

"Shitting dicks, are the farmers farming bodies?!" Arin asked.

"Nah, but it's easier to bury a migrant worker than pay him out," Janet said. "It's sorta like the wild west, cops turn a blind eye. If someone were to start snatching up nobodies, this is a good place to do it."

"Motherfuckers," Arin said. He spat on the grave.

I clenched my fists and spat too. Janet sneered and tossed her joint down before stomping it into the dirt.

• • •

I'd been trying to sleep off my most recent hangover when there came pounding at my door. With bleary eyes and unchanged clothes, I pulled the door open and squinted in sunlight.

Janet.

"Arin said you quit your job." she said. "You okay?"

I winced. I had quit—I still lived at home, it's not like I needed the money.

". . . I was afraid to go outside after I got shot, too," she said quietly.

We sank down on the front steps of my porch.

"Gun misfired and took my jaw halfway off," she said. "My uncle nearly died when I sat up and cussed."

Janet chuckled.

"He's a paranoid mountain man, convinced me to keep quiet. Said the government would wanna vivisect me."

". . . They probably would," I realized.

"I know. I thought it was just me until Arin. I was walking back to the cabin one night when I noticed a car had gone off the bridge. By the time I hiked down and found him, he was twisted up like a pretzel and *still* managed to drag himself thirty yards away from the wreck. Boy doesn't know when to quit."

I kicked the dirt.

"He's lucky he has you," I said.

"You know, you're our friend too, now, Derek. Something like this unites us, you know?"

Janet reached into her pocket and handed me a paper bag.

"This was Arin's idea," she said. "Thought it might help you feel safer."

I took it from her hands and reached inside. A pocket knife. It was obvious Arin had picked it out—the blade and handle were iridescent and shimmering. It was hard not to smile.

It had been a long fucking while since I felt safe.

"You want to come out with us tonight?" Janet asked.

I held the knife tight.

"... Yeah. That sounds good."

• • •

It took a month or two for things to feel normal again. I got my job back, I'd go out drinking with the usual gang on weekends. I still had panic attacks, but Arin taught me breathing exercises, and Janet would hold my hand under the table sometimes when I got quiet. Hanging out with them made it a lot better.

One thing that was different was pain, though, and how it affected me.

It started when I stepped on a nail in the workshop. It went right through my shoe almost out the other side of my foot, but I had to play it cool. If my boss saw he would call an ambulance. It was half an hour before I could take a break long enough to pull it out and bandage it up, and all that time the pain spiraled and twisted inside me. Without the haze of alcohol, it was so sharp. Hurt so long, so bad, that it started to scrape against something in my brain that said—

This feels good.

I stopped drinking as much at home. Just . . . to test things out. With my knife. Probably would have gone farther if I hadn't opened my eyes and saw how much I was bleeding.

NOPE. Not ready to go down THAT road.

I buried it and focused on my new life, on spending time with my strange new friends. Until one night at the bar, Janet's grin faded and her eyes went dark.

"By the door."

I looked at the three sleazy men who just walked in. Arin gasped.

"Fucking fuck," he whispered. "It's *them*."

Immediately, my stomach full of beer soured. They sat down silently in the corner, eyes darting across the bar.

Looking for victims.

I grit my teeth. More than sick, I felt livid.

"Derek, are you—"

"I'm gonna kill them."

Janet blinked at me.

"You don't have to help me," I said, clenching my knife. "But I'm gonna."

"Derek," Arin mumbled. "This is . . . before, that was in self-defense. We only didn't call the cops cuz it woulda outed us."

"You know the cops won't do shit. *We* have to do something." I whispered.

"I'll be bait."

Both our heads swiveled over to Janet.

"I'll make a big show of getting wasted and go outside. I got my hunting knife in my boot. We'll take 'em by surprise on both sides."

She turned to Arin.

"Arin, you can walk out now, and neither of us will blame you."

Arin looked down, brows furrowing.

"... Fuck it. I'm undead. Let's send these sick puppies to Satan."

· · ·

I drove us back to the cabin with three bullets in my back, two bodies stuffed in the trunk, and one sat up in the backseat with Arin. He'd put his sunglasses on it.

It felt good, slicing that hick's belly open while Arin held him, watching his intestines bloom out as the flesh split. Killing was well worth getting shot. And now, feeling my shredded muscle pulse around the bullets, it was starting to feel—

Nope, nuhuh. Not the time.

But as Janet plunged the pliers into my torn back, my toes curled.

That was hard to ignore.

She bent forward to grab me the bottle of whiskey we used to take the edge off last time.

I chewed my lip. Fuck it, I knew I was twisted now. But I didn't know the next time I'd get an opportunity like this.

"... I'm um ... I'm good." I said, trying to keep my voice steady.

I winced, waiting for Janet to comment. She just put the bottle down and slid the pliers back into my wound.

Fuck me.

"Left or right?" she asked.

". . . Left," I mumbled.

Janet cursed and tossed the pliers down.

"This isn't helping. Mind if I use my fingers?"

My brain went soft—I was nodding before I could stop myself.

I tried to keep quiet as Janet dug into me. Tried to swallow down the embarrassing sounds before they could escape my throat. Tried to ignore how hard I was growing in my jeans as she twisted her fingers inside me.

My eyes were shut tight when I felt her breath against my ear.

"Feels that good, huh?" she whispered.

Right as my body tensed, she twisted her knuckles. The jolt that radiated outward made me moan.

". . . Sorry," I gasped.

"S'okay. It's like that for me too."

Janet's nail skimmed across the bullet before boring into neighboring tissue. I was breathing heavy now, there was no hiding it.

"Pain and pleasure come from the same chemicals in the brain," she said, flicking her fingers. "For people like us, who can stay conscious through more pain than any normal person can take? It makes sense that our wires would get crossed."

She finally got a grip on the bullet and yanked it out. I was shaking, whimpering from the loss.

"... More?" Janet asked, tracing the wound.

"Yes," I gasped.

I could practically feel her smirk as she sunk her fingers back into me. I leaned back into her and she braced my shoulders against her chest.

"Here, wait ..."

Janet looped her legs around me from behind--her lips brushed against my ear, teeth scraping my jaw. She trailed her other hand up the front of my chest, and pressed down to push her fingers into me deeper.

And it hurt so fucking good it made my eyes tear and roll back at the same time.

When Janet's movement slowed and I finally came back to myself, I realized the bathroom door was open.

Arin was there. Face flushed and eyes dark.

"I, um. I finished digging the ..." He stopped and swallowed. "I—I'm sorry, can I watch? Please?"

And *fuck,* if that didn't do something to me.

"Yeah," I said, and I think Janet liked that too, because she wriggled her index finger against what had to be a riba, and I lurched forward.

"*Fuck* yeah," I groaned.

Janet hooked her legs around my thighs, spreading them apart as Arin knelt down in front of us. He looked an equal mix of nervous and awed.

"Wow," he whispered, like the sick scene he'd walked in on tumbled out of his spank bank.

". . . You can do more than watch," I whispered. "If you want."

Arin shuddered. I tucked my hand into my pocket for my knife. He didn't hesitate to reach out for it—his palm lingering in mine.

"Tell me what's good for you?" he asked.

Janet bit into my neck, and I whimpered helplessly as Arin took the knife.

• • •

"I think I probably need therapy," I said, hours later.

We'd bathed, and Janet had stitched and dressed my new wounds, and the three of us were now piled on the futon—Janet on my left, Arin to my right. I still felt giddy. Basking in the afterglow.

It's weird, knowing something is objectively reprehensible when it feels absolutely *right*.

"I think society as a whole needs therapy," Arin said, snuggling into me. "All people should always get therapy."

Janet traced my side.

"Immersion therapy?" she suggested.

Arin kicked her under the blanket.

"Horny bitch, calm down!"

I snorted and rolled over.

Janet and Arin fell asleep while I lay still, mind buzzing. I thought of the lives we'd saved by killing those hicks. I thought of my new friends, my new desires. I thought about how when I got home, I was gonna pour out my bottle of Wild Turkey.

I thought about how for the first time in years, I didn't want to numb my wounds anymore—I wanted to feel *everything*. And that thought made me feel warm.

Warm and alive.

VISITING A BOY'S ROOM

by
SHEENA DAREE ROMERO

There aren't flowers in Darnell's yard, just big rocks. He unlocks the door and says, "Take off your shoes." I do as I'm told.

I'm wearing Vans. White Girl Shoes. At Holy Spirit Academy, Black girls wear Lugz, Fila, and Nikes. White girls do Sketchers, Keds, and Vans. Everybody rocks Adidas and New Balances. No one wears Champions. I'd wanted British Knights until Tamika said BK stands for Blood Killers, and if I wore them, I'd be called a Crip. The Vans are a betrayal, but I prefer being outcast over having my ass whooped. The first time I wore them, Tamika let me borrow her aunt's Fashion Fair lipstick. Armed with a crimson-lipped confidence, I forgot I had anything to lose. No one said jack about my shoes. Not to my face.

Darnell picks them up, sticks a hand in each one, and bangs them on the ground. Then he puts them next to his red and black Jordans and sniffs his hands. I hope my feet don't smell all gym, popcorn, and funk.

I'm thirteen. He's fourteen. Days separate us from The Final Summer Before High School, before corn-on-the-cob, the State Fair, fireworks, and rebel night-owl suns. I'm geeked for Kool-Aid popsicles, flip-flops, sleeping in. For becoming the girl I want to be before high school. For having my own Fashion Fair.

I like Darnell. He knows all the answers in history and runs so fast we call him "Sonic."

"You ever wish people wore shoes on their hands?" He's weird. And cute.

"Not really."

"What if you could go around barefoot all the time? Would you?"

"I'm used to shoes."

"Want to see my room?" He grabs my hand.

There's a poster of Tupac over Darnell's dresser. This is my first time in a Real Boy's Room. My cousins don't count. Every other girl I know has gone home with a boy. They've schooled me on blow jobs. I was worried about my braces, but they say you don't use your teeth.

"PlayStation?" he asks.

"Yeah." I hope he has good games.

"*Tekken*?"

"Sweet." I'd rather play *Street Fighter*, but whatever.

Darnell hands me a controller. "You like my room?"

"You have so much stuff." Pretty soon, I'm kicking his butt. Is he letting me win? I press the same key a million times in a row.

"Loser has to suck the winner's toes," Darnell adds while I'm way ahead. He's probably going to start getting more points to beat me. Sucking his toes sounds easier than sucking anything else. I guess. Luckily, I win three levels in a row.

Darnell turns off the console. "Guess I have to suck your toes?"

He crawls to me, peels off my socks with the care of people who reuse wrapping paper. He picks up my foot, brings it to his mouth. I don't know where to look, how to act. His tongue is heavy. If I moan, will it sound ugly? No one at school talks about feet stuff. Did he come up with this on his own? Is this what he likes? Does he want me to feel good? Could he like me? He licks the balls of my feet, my ankles, kisses up my calves, behind my knees. He's mid-thigh. I want to kick but resist. I don't want to have to tell my diary, my friends, that I messed this up.

He sits up. I'm relieved he's taking a break before whatever comes next. I want to say I'm nervous but can't. Why can't I just grow the hell up? If I don't get comfortable with boys now, I'll be even weirder by high school. So weird they'll kick me out of prom, and I'll be the first person that's ever happened to. It'll be all anyone ever remembers about me.

"Why don't you shorten your uniform skirt?" he asks.

"I forgot."

"You forget every day?"

We are not following the plan. In Nina's interactive introduction on being with boys, she straddled me and pressed her lips to mine. I fumbled and ached when we switched places. If I reenact that now, I'll probably fart, burp, and spill Tahitian Treat everywhere. I'll never finish eighth grade.

"You're not into this. We don't have to tell. We can pretend we did other stuff."

"My bad." I want to offer him my summer. But he probably has other plans with girls who are ready.

"It's cool. Wanna play another round of *Tekken*?"

"I sort of want to go home." This, the truth, is not what I mean to say.

"Did I freak you out?"

"Noooo."

"Did it feel good?"

"It tickled."

"Tickled? You're funny, Cairo." He looks at his fingernails. They're neat.

We laugh.

When we get to the front door, he circles my palm and thanks me for coming.

"Someday I would definitely drink beer out of your high heels."

"You love you some feet, don't you?"

"Nah. Wouldn't it be funny if I did, though?" He shrugs.

At home, Grandma is sitting on the porch. "Where you been, baby?"

If she finds out I've been to a boy's house, she'll lecture me about how being fast rushes you through life, taking time you can't get back. Then she'll go on about how she's already too young to be a grandma, let alone somebody's great-grandma. How everybody wants to be grown but nobody wanna pay grown folks' bills. I keep quiet.

"Been waiting on you." She strokes my back.

"I saw Tamika and got caught up talking." Does she notice my socks are missing?

"You just as sweet as you want to be, ain't you? Smart, too. Stay like that forever and always, okay?"

I catch our reflections in the glass door. I don't look like a girl who lies to her grandmother. But maybe I've changed. Our arms tangle. "Yes, Grandma. Forever and always."

THE FRONTIER

by
SEAN SAM

I waited and studied them—the people in the pit. Sometimes they spent hours at the dig site, their bodies appearing and disappearing in the sediment, and sometimes they spent just as long in the blue tent beside their manmade chasm, probably analyzing their findings, pouring over bones, congratulating themselves on discovering what did not belong to them. Their science existed to look backward. I knew about bones too, the depth to make them disappear.

They all were strangers—*bilagáana* scientists in Diné

territory—their tent a homestead on the frontier. And their dig site, miles outside Chinle, was remote. No one watched them except me. They were flecks of white skin in my scope. After three weeks of monitoring, I decided it was time.

I was usually more careful. Three months or more between each self-defense was my normal cycle, four spokes in the wheel of a year. But I didn't know how much longer they would be at the site, and I felt I had a good grasp of their schedule. On Saturday mornings, their party always divided and left one digger alone. That person took a trip into town, their route a two-lane road serried by boundless desert.

After midnight on a Friday, I felt a compulsion to leave my blind, to creep closer to them, so I took my .30-30 to the dig site. My grandad, who I felt always resented me for being half white, went on about how full of life it was here, how Diné can feel ancestors in the junipers on the reservation. The valley was empty of everything except me.

I stood outside their tent and tried to listen to them sleeping, imagining their colorless dreams. The night was cold and cool. I was convinced that if a scientist poked his head out, he would not see me. Beside the tent, underneath a tarp, the skeleton of an ancient being was bubbling to the surface. I saw my hand reaching in the moonlight to raise the canvas. I had no idea what creature lived underneath, but I wanted to take a piece of it with me. Maybe the jaw. Forget the heart or brain—the soft organs don't last. Take the teeth, right where the essence exists. Living in the act of chewing others.

Instead, I moved away from the tent and inspected their truck's wheels. Spike strips were too dangerous to set up—a Native officer had recently died during a police chase nearby. I thought about him flailing to plant the strips, the suspect's headlights overtaking his body, all that white before death.

Yes, a direct shot at one of their tires would work better. I would take aim between their camp and the nearest town—anywhere open and empty.

• • •

The next morning, I lay on the bed of my truck and watched the dig site through the scope of my rifle from at least a mile out. A single shape crept across the desert like an ant over a table, moving with an insect's militaristic purpose, checking their tools, their tarp, their tent. They must have believed they were alone.

When they finished inspections, the settler started their truck and drove along the road. Bringing my rifle into a tighter position against my shoulder, I steadied myself. Then I began my breathing ritual.

My brother, John, taught it to me years ago when we used to hunt elk, long before he ran away to become a deep-sea diver. John said take three deep breaths in and then hold. When you let the last breath out, you visualize a vase, like grandma's pottery. He said the fewer colors on your vase, the better—no details to distract you.

Make it bone white. Then you look inside it, see everything in there, where you are, the field around you. And then empty it. Pour it out, drink it, evaporate it so the white of the vase destroys everything. The fear will disintegrate with it. Nowhere left for it to live.

When I took the last breath, I saw myself prone in the dirt. I saw loose dust hovering, the empty white space between, and then everything froze, congealing like bone in a tar pit. I cleared it all. Like John taught me, I squeezed and did not pull. BANG. Direct hit on the passenger side tire, a beautiful shot on a moving target! Ripping over the lines, shooting up dust, the truck spasmed across the road. One side lifted off the ground, but the driver steadied the vehicle before it tipped. Gradually, the truck lost speed and glided toward the end of the asphalt. The squeal of the wheels took a second to reach me.

I scrambled into the front of my truck and brought it to life. The initial calmness I felt when I thought of John was gone, replaced with the memory of him figuring out what I was, replaced with his judgment. I told myself to pour that out too.

I stepped on the gas. I would greet the stranger before any well-intentioned person could steal my good deed.

• • •

She must have seen me coming in her rearview mirror. By the time I pulled up, the driver—a thin, young woman—had gotten out of her truck and was walking toward me. Her red hair bounced on pale shoulders and her dark sunglasses reflected the desert shrubs and road back to me. She could not have stood much over five-foot-four, tiny compared to me. I slouched a bit to reduce my size.

Unreal. That was the word you could put to seeing someone up close whom you only knew through a rifle scope. Soldiers must have felt it when they shot an enemy from a mile away and found a corpse later. The last time—with the tourist—the feeling had been worse because I watched him much longer before approaching. Still, with this woman it was that same queasy stinging, the sharp sensation of being buried by shale.

She was much younger than I expected—either a student or a prodigy. She tried to smile, white teeth beneath black shades.

"Hey there," she said, her voice wavering, clearly shaken by the accident.

I needed to know whether her cell phone worked, but I had already made a mistake. I took no time to get in character. She seemed ready to speak and my tongue felt like a fossil.

"Hey," I said. My voice was too soft from talking only to myself. I tried again louder. "What's the problem?"

She gestured to the truck behind her. "My tire blew out. And no spare either."

"Have you called anyone?"

She ran a hand through her hair and lifted her phone. "Reception isn't working here."

"Yeah, we're kind of nowhere."

She extended a hand. "I'm Emma."

I shook her fingers. Her touch was soft, nearly imperceptible. A lie though, a gentle infection. She was irradiated by the pioneer spirit, the kind thought long eradicated by the naïve. You can see it when you focus. Look at the side of a mesa out here. Everything smooth and natural from afar. Then get close enough to spot an abandoned uranium mine.

She was dressed casually, with a flannel overshirt tied around her waist. As she moved closer, clouds crawled across the sun, and in the half light, for a moment, she seemed to disappear, her skin gone, leaving only her empty clothes floating toward me. Just as suddenly, she returned, and the unreal feeling hovered farther down the road.

It was around the time of the incident with the tourist that I first addressed this feeling. I dealt with the odd untethering by creating a personal philosophy—my theory of the postapocalypse, and it helped me immensely. The theory went something like this. Anything and anyone can become untethered from time. The bone hunters were continuing their normal lives, normal culture, going to school, stealing and categorizing. But I was a posthumous person, my culture the figment of what it once was, an exhalation leftover from a post-apocalyptic mixture of plague and genocide. I was living in a parallel world in which I was one of the last survivors of that apocalypse. They did not realize this alternate reality existed like a bubble within their own. They believed they could see and hear me, but what they saw was filtered through a membrane, a layer making my existence a plume, colorless. And sometimes, as in a two-way distortion, I also saw them as lifeless vessels. Only through action— violent action—could I smash my hand through that bubble, make the skeleton of my arm flesh again, and let them see me.

Emma's lips were moving, but I wasn't listening. When she paused and stared at me, I realized I had not introduced myself. I told her my Anglo name.

"I've lived around here for years," I said, "and this area always has bad reception. I can give you a ride into town."

The offer was out there. I would trap her in the car and drive her to the same place I took the tourist, the place where John and I grew up, a house without running water.

Emma said, "Well. I'd like to try to return to camp first if that's okay?"

She made her voice rise at the end of her question. Maybe it was a habit women did more than men, especially when dealing with a stranger. But it surprised me coming from a white woman.

"It's probably a shorter distance to town from here," I said. "Is your camp back the other way?"

"Oh no, it's not far. The others will be back soon, and I think they can help."

"Others?"

"Sorry, I didn't explain. I'm part of a paleontology team. We've been digging here—it's all approved by the tribe. We have the permits."

That last sentence was blurted out too quickly. So they had a piece of paper.

"Wow," I said. "A real paleontologist. Will you tell me about it?"

Whenever I was forced to be social, I listened more than talked. If you spend eighty percent of the time asking questions, your guest will tell everyone afterward what a great conversationalist you are. Most want to hear their own thoughts out loud and see another face react to them. And it was easier for me because I felt insecure about talking. My mother never talked to me. So I did not learn our language.

She said, "If you've got an interest, I'm willing to teach. But I would like to return to the camp, if that's okay."

"You got a deal. My truck's not the most comfortable."

"No worries. I spent most of the last month digging in the dirt and sleeping in a bag."

Having secured her desire, her voice grew steadier as we walked toward my truck. The passenger side was unlocked, and she had no issues, despite her stature, with stepping into the cabin. I took note of these things to not underestimate her later. Maybe the frontier spirit or whatever *bilagáana* called it, had invaded her at a young age. Yes, I know I am half white. But digging was a trade at its core—not an existence. We had no similarities.

I got in the driver's seat and fished around for my keys. Then I started the truck. "What got you interested in bones?"

"You can learn so much from them. All sorts of things about the past."

"I guess I'm more about the future. What might be or might have been."

"A good dig can tell us a lot about that, too. Someday, people might recover us the same way. Then they'll see how we lived."

"You think so? I'm not sure."

"Of course they will. I suppose they'll find me on the East Coast. I'm from Baltimore."

"I've been here my whole life."

"You planning on living here forever?"

"No choice. After I die here, I doubt anyone will find me."

"They will," she said. I think she was smiling as if teasing me. Agreeing to drive her to the camp must have disarmed her. "Someone will always be looking. That's just what we do."

"I don't think we would stop on purpose. I'm sure the dinosaurs didn't plan on getting wiped out."

"One day, we'll shoot an asteroid down before it blows us up. Hey, speaking of which, that is exactly what we found!"

I drove and thought of when I would switch directions. On a two-lane road, turning around would trigger every alarm in her body. Maybe she would pull the wheel or bite me.

I asked, "You found an asteroid?"

"No, a dinosaur!"

"A big one?"

"Ah. You know, when I used to work in a museum, no one was interested in the Compsognathus we had. It's about the size of a house cat. The viewers were really low, which always disappointed me. I thought the little one was pretty cute. But our huge sauropod always had groups of kids around it."

"Damn, the little guy must have felt bad."

"Eventually, we had to put him in storage to make way for another exhibit. Not sure what happened to him."

I couldn't pretend to know what a field trip was like. John and I stopped going to school around age seven to help at home. Once or twice a social worker came by, but my mom always drove them off by pretending we were nephews who were just "staying for a bit." Eventually, their visits evaporated.

If you've looked into me more since everything or been curious about my education, I can tell you that the formal aspects came from a small library an hour from our childhood home. I would take any books I could carry. Almost everything else I know came from my brother.

"Now," she said. "What we found in our dig won't be forgotten. This thing is a monster."

● ● ●

While driving toward the camp, I thought about John. It always happened like that. I would get close to making a move and thinking about how disappointed in me he was. Not even disappointed. Scared.

Our old home, where I brought the tourist—where I last saw John—had no real nighttime lighting. Every now and then we would use kerosene lanterns. When the moon was around, spots of white would drop through the holes in the roof and make patterns on my skin. It was something to watch.

The last night I saw him, I thought he was out of town—farther than out actually. He told me he was still working toward getting his commercial diver's license. You can imagine one must travel beyond the rez for that. His brain must have traveled that far, too—to want to do that, you know?

I thought he was gone, so I brought the tourist there. I only learned the tourist's name from his driver's license, but I won't go over that part again, except to say that my method was young.

John came back in that silent sedan of his—or maybe all the blood deafened me—and he saw me with the tourist. There was a lot of yelling and maybe crying, too. I got rid of the settler as fast as I could while John stayed inside. Afterward, my lantern was burned out, and my body ached. I could barely see my hand in front of my face. That was fine. The torn-off scabs from digging always seem different in daylight.

I encountered John in the doorway of our home. He was a shape without feature.

"Don't stand there," I said.

"Why?"

"Bad luck to stand there. You know that."

A traditional female hogan, like our childhood home, has one entrance and one exit.

"What happened to you?" John asked.

"Nothing. This is self-defense."

"I can't be here," he said.

"It's alright."

"I can't be here."

"You're here."

I started to tell him. Why I did it. Why I think I did it. But he said he did not understand. He said he wanted to be as far from this as possible.

I kept talking, telling him my theory of the post-apocalypse, telling him what we had to do, talking until I was no longer sure whether he was there. I heard him breathing. I thought he was still there. But the longer I talked, the more I was not sure.

● ● ●

Emma rolled down her window, and I did the same. There was no point in letting the heat make her uncomfortable.

"Yeah, this find, it's gonna be great," she said. "Definitely a kids-crowding-around piece. So—technically—I'm not supposed to show anyone outside of our research crew. But they won't be back at the camp for an hour or two. When we get there, do you want to see it?"

She leaned toward me, smiling, even gently resting a hand on my forearm.

"Yeah, I want to see it."

Soon, we reached the camp. In the dark, the tent and tarp looked like props on a film set. In daylight, sun fell into every crease and fold, and the wind coming off the canyons made the fabric bend and turn. The dead, their wounds and their expressions, often had the same habit of reanimating in white light.

"You like the outdoors?" Emma asked as I stopped the truck.

"Never really thought of it that way. It's not much of a choice here."

"Right, I didn't mean to offend."

"It's okay."

"Sorry, I get excited about this and say stupid stuff. This is the best, though. It's been my dream since I was little, and now it's really happening and I want to tell everyone about it."

"I think I get it. Felt the same after I bought this truck."

She laughed, and I was reminded how young she was by the sound of her voice. "There's just nothing better than being out here doing what you love."

I was no longer surprised by Emma's chattiness, because I didn't believe she was really speaking to me, as much as speaking to an idea, the idea of a true Native to whom she was reciting the ropes, educating the local with the excited air of someone who has learned a fact—a romantic fact—that she needs to make real by injecting it into others.

In the back of the truck, under a tarp of my own, sat the rifle and the other weapons. Did I love this? I could feel that thick barrier, the membrane of it coiling, the strange heat like craving skin. Yet I was hesitating. The others, the ones in charge, would not approve of her showing me all this. So she must have felt some trust. She was young, maybe too young. Did she understand what she was doing—how she was invading?

I parked a good distance from the site, and we walked the rest of the way together, her leading. I decided I would wait and listen to her. Then I would choose.

She stopped by a wooden box filled with tools. "Have you used a trowel before?"

"I haven't."

"This is mine," she said and lifted a tiny shovel with a wooden handle. She lifted another. "Here, you can borrow this one."

She handed me the tool. I felt her fingers brush against mine.

"The best trowels have their point go into the handle," she said. "If it's welded together, it won't last. I've seen those break in a day, sometimes less. Got my initials carved on the bottom of this one. Never carve your initials into the handle itself because you'll get blisters."

"This tool is so important?"

"Oh hell yeah. After a few digs, a good trowel becomes like an extension of your arm. I'd hate to lose this one."

"I see. I have a few things I feel the same about."

"You need clearance on the handle, too, so you don't scrape your knuckles. A good one can last forever."

I said again, "I have things I feel the same way about."

"Like what?"

"In the truck, I have this old war axe."

"No shit?"

"Yeah. My grandpa passed it to my brother, and he then passed it on to me. It's made from flint and bound with rawhide."

"You'll have to show me that later. Man, this meeting with you worked out well. Could be fate or something. No idea what happened to that tire. But now I get to see a living artifact."

Maybe the axe would have been better placed behind museum glass. Then, no one would ever think of using it. I could be there, too.

"Now for the final curtain," she said.

My mouth was dry, and my lips were shaking. It would be too simple to describe her smile as contagious, and yet I found myself wanting to return it. Look at where she was—especially at her age, an age when I had not yet found direction. There was courage, maybe even greatness ahead, not the kind that I endorsed, but the sort that nevertheless could be admired from a distance. If I could only erase her from my world and set her back into another. She would return, though. I was sure of it—curiosity can have disturbing aspects.

She had me stand on the opposite side of the tarp, and together we folded it back. The sun slid into the pit and lit a massive, fractured spine, at least ten feet in length, the ribs and ridges of it poking like spokes out of the earth, its outline a pulverized question mark. At the top of the spine, a row of spiked teeth divided the dirt. As I moved my face closer toward the pit, I felt a tumbling of years inside me—as if I were time traveling through an invisible portal—a funnel sending me into those jaws.

"Amazing. How long has this been here?" My voice seemed to be sliding through that portal.

"At least 190 million years, probably more."

"And no one has messed with it since then?"

"It's just as it was in the old days. That's what makes it special," she said and looked at me. "Alright, be careful, and you can come closer."

None of her colleagues would appreciate me stepping on their bones, their stolen sacred ground. She was sharing a secret with me, and I felt some bizarre urge to protect that.

I slid into the pit after her, keeping a distance from the find. The earthy smell, deep rock strata in an enclosed space, overwhelmed.

"This," she said, "is *Dilophosaurus wetherilli*. We think. We're not sure yet. Otherwise, this place would be busier."

I thought I saw a twitch of movement. The jaw seemed to clench as if the bones themselves had lost connection with the world, loose of gravity and time, ready to open around me.

"I remember the dinosaur from *Jurassic Park*. Wasn't it smaller?"

"Yeah. They made it spit venom in that movie. Totally inaccurate. The last name came from John Wetherill—a Navajo."

I have learned since that Wetherill was not Diné. Only a frontiersman who befriended us and spoke the language. We must have treated him well. So well that his name slid like a stratum over ours and became the one she knew, the one she thought she understood. She might grant me the same erasure. If I left without taking what I came for, no one would ever say I was a bad guy. I could become a story, a tale for her friends to study and look through.

"When we first started digging," she began, and her voice was clear and loud and seemed to come from everywhere. It made it hard to think. "We thought maybe we'd get some trace fossils. But nothing like this. All the other stuff we have on this creature comes from the Kayenta formation. So, I felt pretty good about being on Navajo territory."

"You didn't worry about being on our land?"

She said, "The tribe has helped us out so much. I don't know if they know how valuable this is. It's amazing what we've been able to take."

"Have you repaid what you've taken?"

I am sure I asked that.

"Here, kneel down," she said, and I crouched beside the jaw. "Take a look at that."

I saw little more than a black mark in the dirt where she pointed. The pit was deep enough for the sun to send odd shadows down, and I had to maneuver myself, twisting my body.

"Just there, look," she said.

I turned again to move my shadow.

You get used to the heat here, but the enclosed space, the smell of her perfume, the sun skipping across my neck, all combined to make me sway. White streaks, like sunlight off bone, rotated around the corners of my vision. I felt that if I passed out, no one would find me for 200 million years.

I said, "They don't disappear, do they?"

"This one is a nightmare to imagine. Probably over 20 feet long when it was alive. More than 900 pounds."

"Even this deep."

"We've never found a complete one of these."

"My brother, John, had this thing he taught me," I said. "Sort of like meditation. When I'm afraid, I can use it to make everything disappear."

"This could get all of us in a book," she said.

"Sometimes it doesn't work."

I believe I said that about John. Maybe John would return when I died. He could bury me far from the hogan. Future beings would find and study me with alien eyes, catalog me beside the ones I took, the ones who took me to the limit of life.

"Who gave you permission for this dig?" I asked.

She said, "That shadow right there is the crest."

I said, "Did they ask me? I don't remember them asking me."

"The crest is so beautiful. I wish I could keep it for myself, you know?"

"I think I know. Do you hear me?"

I must have said that to her.

But she didn't respond. She continued to speak, hands moving in excitement—as if alone.

When I said nothing, she stopped and turned to me and asked with alarm, "Are you okay?"

Her pupils were dilated. I can still look into them.

And when I do, I swear—even though we were in the pit and the memory is impossible—I swear I see all the horizon flowing into her eyes.

I'm reflected there. Right at the edge.

Can you see me?

Ron A. Austin's short stories have been placed in *Boulevard, Pleiades, Story Quarterly, Ninth Letter, Black Warrior Review,* and other journals. *Avery Colt Is a Snake, a Thief, a Liar,* his first collection of linked stories, has received several honors, including the 2017 Nilsen Prize, a 2019 *Foreward* Indies Gold Award, a 2020 Devil's Kitchen Reading Award, a 2020 PEN/Robert W. Bingham Prize nomination, and a 2020 Hurston/Wright Legacy Award nomination. Austin's work has been supported by grants from the Regional Arts Commission, including a 2016 Artist Fellowship. He, his wife Jennie, and son Elijah live in St. Louis. As an Assistant Professor of English at St. Louis University, he facilitates fiction workshops.

Venita Blackburn is an award-winning author of the story collections *Black Jesus and Other Superheroes* (2017), *How to Wrestle a Girl,* (2021), and the debut novel, *Dead in Long Beach, California,* (2024). She is an Associate Professor of creative writing at California State University, Fresno.

"Live Birth" was inspired by my grandmother's life as a midwife in rural Alabama during the mid-20th century or so. There is something matter of fact and gossipy about the piece that mimics the way I was told stories about my grandmother's experiences. There is also a sense of terror that is made to feel ordinary in the description of these women's lives that I wanted to demonstrate.

Erin Brown is a Black, neurodivergent poet and author of horror, fabulist, and fantasy short fiction. She has been published in *FIYAH Magazine, The Deadlands, Fabulist Magazine, The Los Suelos CA Interactive Anthol-*

ogy, *Translunar Travellers Lounge*, the anthology *It Was All a Dream: An Anthology of Bad Horror Tropes Done Right*, and *Fantasy Magazine*, with upcoming work in other publications and anthologies in 2024. Erin received the Truman Capote Literary Trust Scholarship in Creative Writing for spring 2022 and was shortlisted for Brave New Weird 2022. Her poetry featured in the *Our California* poetry project created by the California Arts Council and spearheaded by the poet laureate. You can find her on X/Twitter at @babblebrown, BlueSky @babblewocky.bsky.social, or her author website www.ebrownwrites.com.

"Dog" is a horror story, but it is also a love letter to the great Route 99. This road leads in and out of the Central Valley of California, where I spent so many cozy car rides as a child with my family on our way to visit more family in Los Angeles. Watching the fields and orchards and ponding basins slip past my window, the golden hills in the distance on either side, I would daydream about the many stories that lived alongside that road and beyond. I'd make up such stories, in my head to pass the time between rest stops, and the darkest stories always took

place in the dim of the orchards or up in the hills via The Grapevine Interstate 5. I always wanted to write a spin on a fairy-trap fable, and the unique beauty, loneliness, and wild spirit of the valley seemed a great place to have my charming and dangerous protagonist fall in love, and come face to face with his possible doom.

Caridad Cole is a writer, filmmaker, and visual artist currently residing in Los Angeles. Her poetry has appeared in *Tiger Leaping Review* and *Vocivia Magazine*, and she is the 2018 recipient of three awards by *Words for Charity* for her short stories "Empty Houses" and "In A Town Called Albatross." Caridad most often works in magical realism, a tradition she weaves throughout her multidisciplinary work, as well as in the literary and art magazine she founded in 2023, *Moonday Mag*. In her free time, she rescues secondhand clothing, practices henna, and whispers folktales to anyone who will listen.

"The Rabbit Sisters" is a semi-autobiographical story written in 2021, during a time when (I think) a lot of people were missing their family, their home, and the past. I grew up in a very small, rural town, in a renovated farm house on top of a mountain. Our backyard was dense, wooded land. This setting, along with my enigmatic older sister, appear in much of my art. Working on this piece, I revisited one of my most vivid memories of childhood: discovering that my sister had pushed the screen out of her window, taken our pet dwarf rabbit, and run away to sleep in the woods. Her explanation was simply that she "wanted to be with the deer."

Mvskoke/Scottish author Dr. **Deidra Suwanee Dees** grew up picking cotton in rural Alabama on ancestral Mvskoke land. She descends from Hotvlkvlke (Wind Clan) and follows Mvskoke stompdance traditions. She is author of *Vision Lines: Native American Decolonizing Literature*. She serves as Director/Tribal Archivist at the Poarch Band of Creek Indians and teaches Native American Studies at the University of South Alabama.

"Biracial Identity" came about by my dealing with my own biracial identity. By this story demonstrating the difficulties that biracial children sometimes go through, I thought readers could better comprehend the complexities we face in our adult world.

"Southern Church" came about by my own experience in a southern church in Alabama. I wrote this story to help readers to tap into their childhood imaginations that are often formed in unreal views. "Roberta and Her Cow" was inspired by a story an elder told me about a sick cow. The story shows our connection to the natural world through the animals and the importance of protecting the natural world through medicine and healing.

Jessica (Mehta) Doe, PhD, is a multi-award winning Aniyunwiya inter/multi/anti-disciplinary poet, artist, and scholar. As a citizen of the Cherokee Nation, space, place, Indigenization, and de-colonization are the driving forces behind her work, which includes several books and exhibitions. Her doctoral work addressed the meeting point of eating disorders and female poetics. During her post as a Fulbright Senior Scholar in Bengaluru, India, she curated a poetry anthology in the colonizer's tongue. She is the current Bayard Rustin artist-in-residence in Manhattan, a 2023/24 Peace Studio Fellow, the Lead Poet-in-Residence at New York's Kristine Mann Jung Library, and the forthcoming 2024 BigCi

Environmental Award fellow in Australia. Visit www.thischerokeerose.com for more information.

This story began as part of a short story exercise. I am mostly a poetry writer and artist. However, Indigenization and decolonization are driving factors in all of my work, including prose. My goal is to share stories, perspectives, and experiences from an Indigenous lens. For many Indigenous people, the lines between "reality" and so-called mis-truths are blurry and ever-changing, but also a means of connecting to our ancestors, ourselves, and our history.

Mark Ennis lives and works in Maine. When he's not practicing as a registered nurse, he spends his time exploring nature, shopping for records, and writing.

I was having a conversation years ago with my father's cousin, Dan, an elder who had devoted most of his life to Native rights. Dan loved to tell stories about his life but on one occasion, he told me about a dark incident from his childhood involving an Indian agent that would harass his family. They lived on a reserve in rural Canada, just north of Maine, and during one win-

ter his father was arrested by the Indian agent for chopping wood without permission. He was locked in a shed for five days for this "crime". Eventually, Dan's family had to leave the reserve under duress as the harassment from the agent increased. Dan passed away a few years ago but this story continued to deeply resonate with me. When I was a child, I felt trapped in a situation I couldn't escape from, with little opportunity to express myself or communicate my concerns. I wrote "The Axe" from the perspective of a child, to allow their voice to flourish with full agency as they embark on a journey of discovery.

Jane Hammons taught writing at UC Berkeley for many years before returning home to New Mexico. She has work forthcoming in *Brilliant Flash Fiction*, and her writing appears in numerous magazines and anthologies: *Alaska Quarterly Review, Southwestern American Literature, and The Yellow Medicine Review, Hint Fiction* (W.W.W. Norton) and *The East Over Anthology of Rural Writers* (EastOver Press). She is an enrolled citizen of the Cherokee Nation.

In 2000 when George W. Bush was elected by the Supreme Court to the presidency of the U.S., I worried he would carry out Reagan's promise to overturn *Roe v. Wade*. I began revising an abandoned novel to remind myself and readers what life was like for women before *Roe*. *Border Crossing (1963)* is an excerpt from that still unpublished novel.

Much of my fiction is inspired by political situations, and it's always challenging to write such stories without heavy-handed exposition. Laurie's border crossing is based on a story my mother told me about driving a friend of hers to El Paso. They were both young single mothers (my mother 30, divorced after 14 years of marriage, with 4 children), and Mom thought they were going to Juárez to kick up their heels. At some point during the night, someone picked her friend up from the motel and didn't return her until the next morning. Unbeknownst to Mom, she had driven her friend to the border for an abortion: illegal in both the US and Mexico.

Growing up near the border in the days before *Roe*, these stories were common. More than one girl I knew in high school died from complications following an unsafe abortion. I was thrilled when *So to Speak*, a femi-

nist journal published at George Mason University, published the story in Summer 2022 and nominated it for a Pushcart Prize. The Supreme Court overturned Roe with the Dobbs decision that same summer. We are now witnessing the consequences of that decision, so, while the situation does not make me happy, the inclusion of the story in this anthology does.

Soon Jones is a Korean lesbian writer and poet originating from the rural countryside of the American South. Their work has been published in *Writers Resist, The Good Life Review, Juke Joint, Moon City Review,* among others, and is currently pursuing an MFA in Poetry at Oklahoma State University. They can be found at soonjones.com.

Back in 2013, I wrote the first draft of "Downburst" in my journal at 2:30 a.m. It sat on shelf for years before I dusted it off and revised it, based on my own surreal experience returning to the farm I once lived on that had since been sold to a paper mill. I'm always thinking about how both cultural and physical isolation in a rural community shifts the kinds of dangers you come across in the country, especially when you're the only non-white person around, and all the different secrets that get buried. It's so easy to go "missing" and never be found. For "Downburst," I wanted to take one of those secrets and bring it to light, with that country version of justice I grew up with.

Kasimma is from Igboland. She's the author of *All Shades of Iberibe*. Her short stories, essays, poems, and scripts appear in *Guernica, Solarpunk, LitHub, New Orleans Review, Meet Cute, Mangoprism, The Saltbush Review, The Forge, Afreecan Read, Native Skin, Writers Digest,* and other online journals and print anthologies. Kasimma is an alumnus of Chimamanda Adichie's creative writing workshop, Wole Soyinka Foundation writers' residency, and others across Lebanon, Senegal, Spain, and the United States. You can read more of her pieces on her website: www.kasimma.com.

I first read about *igwọ ike ji ndụ* in J.A. Umeh's two volumes of *After God Is Dibia*. I was also, still am, in love with Theresa Onuorah. So, while visiting my sister in Georgia, among the many things we discussed, she told me about the last days of her friend who stayed in a coma for a long time, who would umm (still in a coma) when the

nurses tried to clean his body or even touched him, and who suddenly (still from the depths of coma) scratched his neck in such a vicious way it scared his visitors. How, pray tell, could a near-dead man scratch his neck? The doctors said it was something called reflex. Two nights after that gist, I did not bat an eyelid until I had written every 6000 words (who counts punctuations?) of "Healthy Heart" first draft.

Arah Ko is a writer from Hawai'i and the author of *Brine Orchid* (YesYes Books 2025) and *Animal Logic* (Bull City Press 2025). Her work has appeared in *American Poetry Review, Ninth Letter, The Threepenny Review, New Ohio Review,* and elsewhere. Arah was nominated for Best of Net and Best New Poets and received her MFA in creative writing from the Ohio State University. Arah edits at *Surging Tide Magazine* and is pursuing her Ph.D. in English at the University of Cincinnati. Catch her at arahko.com.

I am constantly trying to unbraid the complicated relationship between trauma and memory. There is a blurriness to recollection, to the plasticity of the brain, that verges on the surreal, so that sometimes, real life is more unbelievable than fiction. "Camaro" is inspired by, and blends together, multiple "true" stories—including a bloody encounter I had at 2am at a Waffle House in Kentucky—while contributing to the long and fraught relationship between American fiction and the road. Cars are such an iconic and problematic American icon. I was inspired by the grungy, impoverished, resilient, colonial, and familial backdrop of endless American highways that feel omnipresent in both my own life and media, from Laura Ingalls Wilder to Cormac McCarthy to The CW's *Supernatural* (2005-2020). There is an inescapable resemblance to *Supernatural* in my short story: in the TV show, two brothers travel rural American fighting literal demons in a '67 Impala, while in my piece, two young boys escape metaphorical demons in an '81 Camaro. Today, an increasing number of unhoused Americans do live in their cars as a last, desperate option. The pervasive second person in this piece adds an unnerving, nearly prophetic edge as it invites the reader to see the whole world through a young narrator who measures every experience in terms of the vehicle he calls home.

Like most fiction, "Chicken Husbandry" starts with the truth. My transplant upbringing in a rural, agricultural region of the Big Island in Hawai'i bears a close resemblance to the speaker's: as a young teen I did raise, breed, butcher, and consume my own chickens, and I experienced a complicated range of feelings about the process, and the intersections with farming, colonialism, and gender, as hinted at in this piece. But beyond these resemblances, this story was my reaction to a kind of harsh and reductive veganism and general approach to animals that I encountered in pristine suburban collegiate environments. Although I hold great admiration for many tenants of veganism, the way many of my classmates experienced creatures – from betta fish to birds to feral cats and laboratory fetal pigs – felt artificial, even naïve, reducing complex ancestral relationships with animals, rural life, and even Native practices, into something reprehensible while simultaneously partaking in harmful environmental systems without flinching. My hope in writing this piece was to share a bit about my own experience with animals, and how farming can be, at once, hard, disgusting, brutal, beautiful, respectful, necessary, culturally relative, and instructive.

Joe Milan Jr. is a second-generation Korean American and the author of the novel *The All-American* (W.W. Norton). His work has appeared in *Electric Literature, Literary Hub, The Rumpus,* and others. Read more of his work at joemilanjr.com.

Growing up near Seattle, every summer was "Seafair." There were speedboat and milk carton boat races on the Puget Sound and in the lakes. I remember little replica Viking boats. I don't remember them so much in Seattle, but on my side of the Puget Sound, in a little town of Poulsbo, where the Viking warship adorned Poulsbo bread and every sign and building I can remember.

For Koreans, I never saw Yi Sun-sin's Turtle ship in America, yet in Korea, that kind of warship adorns many things: restaurants, museums, and fishmongers. To me, there is something in one kind of old-world military history of raids and piracy being a celebrated marker of heritage in a new world while others seem absent. What if someone did all they could to assimilate, including embracing another history? Would it become their own just because they wanted

it to? "Oarsmen Wanted" is just one possibility of that idea.

Jacob Anthony Moniz (he/him/his) is a writer and visual artist from California. He holds degrees from UC Santa Cruz, NYU, and the University of Notre Dame. His writing has appeared in *Catamaran Literary Reader, Penumbra, Chicago Quarterly Review, The Ocotillo Review, The Whisky Blot,* and *Southeast Review,* among other journals and publications. For the 2023-2024 cycle, Jacob was a Fulbright Student Researcher working on a creative nonfiction project at the University of the Azores in Portugal. A book connecting his family history to topics of the Azorean diaspora is forthcoming.

"To Keep the Mind Quiet" was developed during a workshop with John Straley at the Catamaran Writing Conference in 2015. I was an undergraduate creative writing student at UC Santa Cruz at the time and had just begun writing a series of short stories set in California's Central Valley. Fresh on my mind were ideas related to life in the Central Valley, topics specific to that area I felt that popular literature had overlooked. When

I workshopped the piece with John Straley, he was concerned, thinking I had mistakenly submitted memoir in place of fiction. I considered his response an incredible compliment. I held onto the story for years before eventually finding it a home in *The Ocotillo Review* in 2022.

Rachel Nussbaum is a mixed-race writer and artist from the Big Island of Hawaii. Her short story *Whiskey to the Wound* was originally published in *Brewtality* from Evil Cookie Press and was reprinted in *Year's Best Hardcore Horror Volume 6* from Red Room Press. Rachel's short fiction and poetry have been featured in many anthologies, including *The Mammoth Book of Dieselpunk* from Running Press and *Crash Code* from Blood Bound Books. Her debut novella *We Rotted in the Bitterlands* came out in 2021 from Mannison Press, and will hopefully be the first of many more longform projects for her. Rachel currently resides in the Bay Area, where she hopes to grow her creative career and one day write and illustrate her own novels and comics.

"Whiskey to the Wound" was originally inspired by a prompt for sick and twisted romance, but it quickly turned into a story more about a very weird yet sweet kind of friendship. The backwater setting is very much taken from my own experience, both from growing up on a rural island and from the time I spent living in the woods of Mendocino County. I think anyone who grew up in a small town or in the country knows how isolating it can be; especially when you're a young adult and it feels like you might really get stuck there forever. Forever isn't so hopeless when you've got people in your corner who know what you've been through, though. I love the dynamic between Derek, Janet and Arin and I'm currently working on more stories with them.

sheena daree romero is an essayist, humorist, and doodler based in NYC. Her stories and essays have been awarded the Miriam Chaikin Prose Writing Award, featured on the *Longreads* "Best of 2022" list, and published in *Autostraddle, Passages North, Taco Bell Quarterly*, and elsewhere. JUST RIGHT, her essay-collection-in-progress, bridges travel memoir, cultural criticism, and found material to meditate on blackness in disparate locations.

"Visiting a Boy's Room" first appeared in *Split Lip Magazine's* 2021 Summertime special issue edited by Tyrese Coleman. It came about from a hope to depict some of the sweet awkwardness that comes with having a middle school crush.

Sean Sam is a member of the Navajo Nation and an MFA candidate at Cornell University. His writing has appeared in *Joyland, Salt Hill, Poetry Northwest,* and elsewhere. He is the winner of *Terrain.org's 12th* Annual Fiction contest, received an honorable mention in *Zoetrope: All-Story's* Short Fiction Competition, and was a finalist for *Poetry Northwest's* James Welch Prize.

This story began with questions: what if there was a terrorist who decided to enact violent retribution for the genocide of indigenous people? What would they be like, what would they believe? Could I present their views in a way that was not exploitative? I wanted this story to create an inversion of the usual "victim" narrative, forcing the reader into a new and uncomfortable space.